*Reloaded Version 2013*

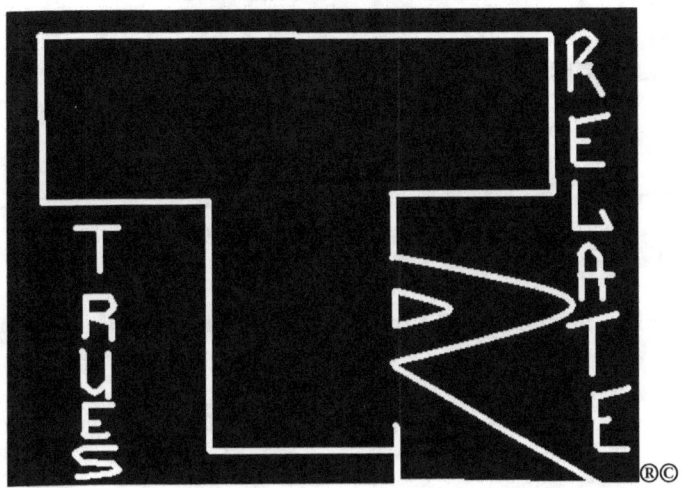

## MORE THAN 4 ADMIRERS-RELOADED©
### "The Threat to a Legacy"
### A Time Will Reveal short story #1
### By Black Coffee©

# MORE THAN 4 ADMIRERS-RELOADED

Published by True's Relate Publishing
[MORE THAN 4 ADMIRERS-RELOADED]
"A Threat To A Legacy!"
Time Will Reveal short story 1
Library of Congress Control Number:
Copyright ©2011 True's Relate publishing/LTBROWN

REGISTERED TRADEMARK-MARCA REGISTRADA
ISBN:978-0-9844701-5-0
Printed in the United States of America
Set by: Createspace
Cover design by : Gregory Spencer of Misvision Graphics
info@misvisiongraphics.com
Logo design: JayRocOne [@ age 15] JayRocOne Designs]

Requests for information on ordering, scheduling the author for signings
and
appearances should be addressed to:
**Black Coffee's websites**
www.truesrelatepublishing.com
http://www.blackdollone.com
On Facebook: Black Coffee
Facebook group: Black Coffee's Crew Nation-The Movement
http://Twitter.com/AuthorBlkCoffee


Manuscript Preparation: Black Coffee
True's Relate publishing company
P.O. Box 2911
Gulfport, Ms. 39505
blackdollone@att.net


## II

# MORE THAN 4 ADMIRERS-RELOADED

## PUBLISHER'S NOTES

# MORE THAN 4 ADMIRERS-RELOADED

Dedicated to the diehards and book junkies who love the Time Will Reveal series!

==================

## The Time Will Reveal short stories

### #1 MORE THAN 4 ADMIRERS!
"The Threat to a Legacy"

### #2 MR. WRONG AND THE RATS
"Sweet Ray, Sonya, Shuntay & Tina"

### #3 THE CREW'S PRIORITY[TBA]
"The Crew Ladies"

### ORDER THE FULL SERIES AT:
www.truesrelatepublishing.com

## The Time Will Reveal-the novel series

Time To Learn-RELOADED-part 1
Time To Grow-RELOADED-part 2
Time To Love-RELOADED-part 3
Time To Know-RELOADED-part 4
Time To Feel-RELOADED-part 5
The Making of AJAY-Every Man (Print only)
Time To Show-RELOADED-part 6 [TBA]
Ajay and Ebony 1-Time Will Reveal 7-Time To Give [TBA]
Ajay and Ebony 2-Time Will Reveal 8-Time To Live [TBA]

# MORE THAN 4 ADMIRERS-RELOADED

## MORE THAN 4 ADMIRERS-RELOADED
### "The Threat To A Legacy!"

It's the day after Christmas 1990. The same day one of the beloved crew named Cheston "Stoney" Coleman had been gunned down in his home and pronounced dead later at East General hospital. As they sat around Chill's home trying to make sense of it all, the crew got word that Stoney's mother, Jackie Coleman Carr had just arrived from Columbus to make preparations for her son's *homegoing*. Chill told all of the females to go over to mama Deb's to assist their mothers with the arrangements. The men needed to talk in private. Ebony didn't want to leave Ajay's side but he insisted she go. It took some convincing but she finally left with Bre and the young ladies. They headed to Bre's house to see what they could do to help their mother's with arrangements for Stoney's final rest.

Once they were gone, the guys got down to the brass tacks and as usual, Chill took the lead. It was time for them to discuss an issue that was only talked about amongst the men in the crew family. *The Big Jake beef.* The older ladies knew of this beef situation and had known for quite some time. Only because it was as old as some of them. But the females in Chill's generation know nothing of it and they won't know unless the time comes to make them aware. That time would be when they become mothers. This way they will understand why certain things are the way they are and why the sons in the family have to be allowed to grow up early. There's a target on their backs. One they all inherited just by being born into the crew family. Namely a Jackson, a Payne or a Williams. But most recently, Jackson and Payne. It has spawn for decades and shows no signs of going away. The fellows are always reminded of it. But losing one of their own isn't the usual. And certainly not at the hands of their enemy. But this time it was and it isn't something they're going to take lightly.

"This is not random and we know it," Chill said and his guys agreed.

"This came from this Johnson family beef, we've known about all of our lives."

"Lil Jake was in that car last night," Jb said.

Chill said, "I saw him and I told y'all then, we wasn't crossing no lines to sale to him. I told Stoney to double up, last night. But he didn't feel like it was necessary."

"I tried to get Stoney to let me stay there but he wanted everybody to leave," Rob said, "Even Bre."

"He was feeling down," Tank added, "I noticed it and asked if me and Nina boo could stay over but he was like, *'Nah bro. I'm good.'* So we didn't push him. I wish we would have."

"I did," Rob said, "But he wasn't having it."

"Thing is," Chill said, "as guys in this crew we're privy to this information that our females don't have. We're their protectors. Renee knows because she's my son's mother. Tonya will be told as well but only after the baby comes. Only us men need to be told of these Johnson situations. That old bastard will never give up. All of us in this room know this shit has gone on since the fifties. Since our grandfathers was our age."

"And if it's all the same to y'all," Ajay said, "I would like to end this shit before I'm a father. Because I'm not trying to see that old ass motherfuckah get lucky enough to kill me or my son. And not my pops, for damn sho."

"He got both of my parents," Chill said, "And don't think for a minute that I don't know that bitch is trying to take me too. But we're definitely gonna shank his old ass. We're just bidding our time and lining up some real powerful allies. When everything is in place, his ass is going in a hole."

6

"Without a service and the church music," Rich adds.

"He wants me worse than he wants you, bro," Ajay said to Chill, "He holds a grudge against both of my grandfathers and my pops too. I mean, like this old fucker is *really* stupid wit this shit. The only way to kill it is to kill *him*."

"And everyone who's associated wit him," June added.

"He holds that grudge against my grandfather too," Chill said, "But you're right. He would love to kill a Jackson or a Williams man. He got a hard-on for you, Ajay. For real and as head of this crew, that shit will not go down."

"He knows for a fact that Stoney's dad didn't killed his son," Jr said.

"Yea he knows Chester Lee took one for the team," Rob said, "His team took my daddy but why did he go at Stoney?"

"Any crew member is a feather in his cap," Jb said.

"I feel he did it because he couldn't get to Ajay or Chill," Jr said, "And maybe he felt disrespected that the crew got someone showing that much love that he would go to prison to save a Jackson. That's why they went at him today. But we all know they want to take out a Jackson, Payne or a Williams first. And not one of us is gonna take that old fart lightly."

"My pops and big John killed Jake Jr," Ajay said, "And I'm gonna kill him and his grandson, so help me God. That bitch wants to kill me because my grandfathers wasn't no suckers. I wanna fuck his ass up and down. I usually don't mess with senior citizens. But that one there, I'll make an exception for."

"Oh he sent his statement in the mail to *Crew Details* and to addresses where he knew our family of fathers would see it. His statement clearly showed he still wants to kill Ajay and everything that keeps him going."

7

"*He's going to make the pro's, one day if we don't kill him first. But even before he can go pro, if he lives that long, he'll have to attend college. Which means he'll need to leave the nest and his love. That's when we'll infiltrate his cushion. Make his bed as hard as a rock. Tear him down from the inside, like his bastard grandfathers did me. I told y'all this vendetta goes deep. While Ajay is away, we need to show his girl how to play. Because that's the one thing that'll surely bring him down. The need for the women in their lives to be faithful, is the backbone of the men in that family. They was fine with my family being torn apart. My women cheating too. So if we can rip the virtue from that sheltered one who's being groomed for Ajay. The one they all tend to protect. Then one by one, the rest will fall. Her father helped his father to kill my son. I feel deeply about that concept. Ajay is the golden boy and she's the princess of their next generation. When I remove them, they'll be devastated. That'll end their family's dominance right along with their "we can rule the world" attitude. They're the reason my sister ran off with that white boy. And they cheated me out of property that in all rights, could've still been partly mine. But I fell on hard times and couldn't make the rent. They refused to carry me and pay my bills, like they did for each other. That could've been done easily but they wouldn't. They offered me a source but I couldn't be okay with no white man holding my deed or securing it. He wouldn't give me a job in his company, so why would I trust him? But he hired that sheltered ones father and it was their crew who took my son's life. Then that white man protected them with a scapegoat who agreed to do the time. I never trusted Jeb Baker. I wasn't gonna let him into my life, so Jeb along with that crew, took my sister, my son and my livelihood. The only way to have my life back is to take theirs and that's what I'm gonna do.*"

8

# MORE THAN 4 ADMIRERS-RELOADED

That statement had come from the mouth of Mr. Jacob Denard Johnson Sr better known as big Jake. The uncle of Carl and Craig Griffith and the grandfather of none other then, Jacob "Jake" Denard Johnson III.

Jake III was 1 of the 3 assailants who had taken Stoney's life. Craig was 1 of the admirers who approached the foursome at *Richmond Town Square mall*, on that beautiful and bright spring day in 1992. It was Carl who, while another 1 of his homeboys drove his blue and white Regal, sat atop his passenger door and unloaded a semi-automatic weapon into the bodies of Chill and his then, pregnant wife Renee in 1993. As they left the mall, after shopping for décor for their little girl's nursery. Carl, Craig and Jake III are all deceased now. In Jake's case, so are his 2 cohorts. The partners of the others don't have as long to live as they may think, because the crew never fails to clean up.

Big Jake had made many attempts on the lives of members of the Cleveland crew and he was successful in some of his endeavors. He had plotted and been successful in causing the tragic automobile accident which took the life of Mrs. Willamena Wright-Payne in 1979. He had also set up the shooting in 1988, where her husband, Paul Jr or big Paul was shot and perished, some weeks later. Willamena and Paul Jr was the parents of big Chill, the target of the failed hit in 1993. Chill is the leader of the 3rd generation of the crew which had long been the target of big Jake's hate. None of the hometown attempts on the lives of crew members was random except for one. The one done by Angel Taylor. She had no background about the beef between these families, which was generated by big Jake. Hers beef was about getting some of Ajay's beef. But she may be recruited, now that she's incarcerated. Because her crew strike was big news. Big Jake was known to scout out and

9

bring in anyone who had hatred for *any* member of the crew. He would even provide the tactics, the plans and plots plus the extra manpower too, if necessary. Anything that would help to carry out his agenda of killing off those he deemed to be his enemies.

Stoney's killing wasn't random, in the least. Neither was any of the rest of them. Stoney was the first successful hit against Chill's crew, however. But he wasn't the first attempt and it surely won't be the last.

Eddie Washington was the first one big Jake was able to get near the crew through infiltration. He had gotten in by pretending he wanted to sell drugs for Chill and be down with the crew. Something that many folks had done and still do. But not because they're trying to kill a member of the crew. That was Eddie's angle. Set-up and monitored by big Jake.

The plot and plan big Jake had sent him in with, was to get in and find out what he could about where the crew kept their products. He was to report it back to big Jake, who would in turn tell the police and get as many members of the crew arrested and jailed, as possible. He had done that during the civil rights pilgrimage which had cost many of the crew friends their freedom and in some cases, their lives. But here is the reason Eddie's plot was unsuccessful.

The crew has a better system of communication than big Jake. They've had it since the days of Allen Saul, Allen Devante Sr and Paul Sr. Even though the crew suffer a fatality, every now and then, they haven't suffered nowhere near the loses they have dealt to big Jake.

"I want you all to make sure and get that egg headed negro named Ajay," big Jake had said to Jake III, Greg Harrison, Eddie and Danny Washington.

That was a few months prior to Ebony and Tank's trip to big

10

mama's, in 1989. Eddie thought he was in by the beginning of that summer but he wasn't. He was to try and get Ajay alone by pretending that someone had shorted him on money for drugs. *Chill's drugs.* He was planning to have Ajay ride with him to confront the thieves. The non-existent thieves. The plan was to take Ajay to a spot off Puritas Avenue where Jake III, Danny and Greg would be waiting to shoot him. Ajay was the 1st option of crew members to target because big Jake sincerely hated both of his grandfathers. But if they couldn't get Ajay, then Chill was the next option. However, any dead crew member would suffice for big Jake. The crew had been correct with their assessment of big Jake's pecking order.

"Now that he's got that girlfriend," Eddie had told big Jake before he was dropped off at Gordon Park for the hit attempt, "He don't really hang out and bullshit, no more. He spends most his spare time with her. Either at her house, Chill's house or they play basketball at the court. But *all* of the crew be there, when they go somewhere and she don't ever go nowhere alone. Her girls are always with her. There is always at least four of them."

Once he found out Ajay had a girl, that's when big Jake decided he wanted to target Ebony. He wanted to cut Ajay as deep as he possibly could, before he killed him. Ironically, the attack that happened to Ebony in Houston had nothing to do with big Jake. But he planned for a similar attack on her, in Cleveland. That's where Craig and Carl's friend, Tim Murphy came in. He was suppose to build up her trust in him, get her to go out with him regularly and then he was going to beat her up and rape her. It wasn't anything against Ebony, personally. Big Jake just figured that would've been a good gut punch for Ajay. One that would certainly weaken him, somewhat so he could catch him off his P's. Big Jake just never understood

11

how deep the layers are in which the male crew come with.

While he was teaching his offspring to hate, try to kill or outdo the crew, the crew matrons kept surveillance on him. That way they could tell the young men under them what to expect. Thus Chill's crew usually had some type of heads up. They didn't always know the names or faces. But on most attempts, they had some type of knowledge before an attack happened. The crew was trained as young as eight years old. They earned street tenure with each generation. By the time Chill's crew was active, the majority of their information came directly from the streets. Info from loyal folks who'd been loyal for generations, even and especially the incarcerated. Big Jake is not nearly as deep but still he tries and often loses.

"We're gonna take them bastards out, one at a time, if we have too," big Jake said for years.

But every time he went after the crew, he lost at least 1 of his own soldiers. That was evident when Eddie went to the chamber. Here's the inside scoop on the summer of 1989 and the plot that was set up and attempted, 18 months before Stoney was eventually killed.

"We're heading out to Gordon park, in a few," Chill had said to his crew.

It was that afternoon after big John had left with Ebony and Tank, heading to Houston.

"That info we got on Eddie, awhile back," Ajay said, "Today is the day he's suppose to make a play on me. So y'all already know I gets to split his dome."

"Son, I don't want you to underestimate this dude," Al had said, "Even though their chief is a dumb ass. Still, I want y'all to be tactical when you go out there."

"We will, big Al," Jb said, "We're gonna flank him."

They all loaded up in their vehicles. The females are to come

12

after the guys have made their move. Chill goes to his back porch to let Renee know they're about to go on that errand and what her part is in the whole scheme of things. She has to make sure she gets her role down precisely. For this is going to be apart of her man's alibi, if the need should arise.

"So baby, I know you want us to wait until later," Renee said to Chill, "What time do you want us to head out there?"

"An hour after dark," he'd told her.

The guys had gone out to Gordon Park and caught Eddie before he could alert his back up. He had tried to stall but he knew the crew wasn't going to allow him to linger. Being that Eddie had no idea they were on to him. Nor did he have any knowledge that the crew knew he was a plant, he got into the Blazer with them and figured he could talk his way into another chance. The crew had already given him 2 chances to pay up the money he owed. They just played along, since he seemed determined too. Thing is, he hadn't honored either of the 2 chances they had already given him. There wasn't going to be a third. That night, he died at the chamber at the hands of the crew member he was suppose to set up. And Ajay asked and was granted the deed of doing him in. Being that it was only his birthright. Ajay had asked to do him for 2 reasons. One was because he had missed out on the 6 squatters at their warehouse, the week prior. They wasn't a part of the Johnson beef. The was just some disrespectful ass clowns who had set up shop on crew territory and wasn't paying any rent. But the main reason Ajay wanted to be the 1 to kill Eddie was because he knew the whole plot in which Eddie was attempting to carry out, was put together out of hate for his blood, his genealogy and his foundation. He did Eddie in with no hesitation and he actually seemed to have enjoyed it.

13

# MORE THAN 4 ADMIRERS-RELOADED

After Ajay took Eddies life, the crew went back to the park. First of all, they wanted to see if his accomplices would show. If they had shown up, they would've invited them to some action too. Eddie's help never showed but his girl did. She showed up looking for him. That was the part of the kill Ajay and his crew loved dearly. His girl's name was Nicole. She came out looking for Eddie but he was ghost. So Ajay, knowing what big Jake's crew had planned for Ebony, decided to partake in Eddie's girl. Nicole was more then willing to fuck another man. That was something Ebony wouldn't ever do and Ajay knew that, with certainty. So once they was clear on what was going to go down, Ajay drove Nicole's car and put Rich in the back seat with the stash girl from last week. The one Jr had fucked, less than a week ago. Her name was Angie and she was rumored to be dating Lil Jake, at the time. That didn't matter none because Ajay and Rich traded and used Nicole and her good friend Angie, at the unused baseball field which wasn't too far from their neighborhood street. Once they got there and got out of the car, where they could have more room, Ajay and Rich fucked them every which way but loose. Then they switched them up and fucked the other one. Ajay kept his trick next to the car while Rich went to the dug out with Angie. This was when they 1st got there. Ajay had no patience nor real interest in Nicole. But it was a possible nut and his girl was on the highway headed to Texas.

"How do you want this dick, bitch?" Ajay asked Nicole, very impatiently but he didn't allow her to tell him.
Instead he told her, "You're gonna suck this motherfuckah or we can just head on back. I don't do no fuckin unless I get my dick sucked, real good, first. So tell me, are you good with these lips?" he asked as he ran his fingers around the outline of her juicy mouth.

14

# MORE THAN 4 ADMIRERS-RELOADED

She was hot for him and she tried to kiss him, several times. "And don't try to kiss me, no more. I don't kiss ho's. Don't no girl kiss me unless it's *my* baby girl. These lips of mine are for Ebony Brown. Understand me when I say that."

"I wanna suck you off," Nicole told him, "But without the condom."

"Bullshit," Ajay said, "Suck it like this or we're heading back to my brother's house."
She got on him and sucked him just like it was lips to skin. Then once he got a nut, she asked if she could drink his semen. "Fuck no," he said, "Damn you nasty as *fuck*. I need to have you marketing this ass for me. You wit that?"

"I just might be," she had said.
He pulled a fresh condom on and shoved his dick into her while bending her over the back of her trunk. She was loving it. He was ramming her with his entire 13 inches of dick and she was making lots of noise. She didn't even want him to stop when Rich and Angie returned. She seemed turned on when she noticed them watching. Angie was turned on too. It was then that the guys switched them up.

By the time they were done tricking, Nicole and Angie was committed to making money for Ajay. He just had it like that. They got in the car and had the girls to drop them back at Chill's house and move on.

Once inside and seated comfortably, Ajay commented on the events of the day and the evening.

"Eddie's ass needed to die," he said, "He ain't even man enough to keep his woman from straying. He was a bitch made nigga."

"Yep. Now all we need is a lead on who the rest of his pack is," Jr said, "We know Jake the third is one of 'em. But we need the other names and we need their ho's names too."

15

# MORE THAN 4 ADMIRERS-RELOADED

"That'll just be more ho's to fuck," Stoney had said and they all laughed.

"I like when we fuck they ho's in front of them, though," Ajay said, "Before they die, we make 'em watch us fuck they bitches. That's crew shit, right there. That's how y'all brought me in, back in the day.

If the crew *had* had a lead on the other 3 guys on that July night, they could've done away with them then. Thus they wouldn't have been around to do the hit on Stoney, a year and a half later.

Eddie's accomplices had shown up at the park but they had come right before Renee and the girls got there. Nobody knew their faces yet. Jr, Rob and Stoney was still at the park, along with the crew females. Eddie's team wasn't willing to make themselves known, right then. They hadn't gotten a call from Eddie, so they went back to the west side of Cleveland to tell big Jake and let him regroup.

But even before Eddie non-return from Gordon park, big Jake already knew he was dead. He knew it because he knew how the crew did things. The crew always got the jump on big Jake. He had to come up with another plot, real soon. He changed his game plan, re-employed the accomplices, then deployed his next set of workers. The hit on Stoney was originally for Ajay and then, Chill. Big Jake sent his grandson Jacob III or Jake, Eddie's brother Danny and their gang brother Greg Harrison.

Unlike the crew, big Jake and his followers were gang affiliated. They needed to be, in order to get enough people together who was willing to be foes of the Cleveland crew. Big Jake has tried every angle known to man to infiltrate the crew and none of them has worked, too date.

There was a reason Eddie had failed to be hired as a

16

loyal worker, even before the info on him was revealed to Chill and his crew. It was because he was to dumb to realize he had to show good faith to the crew by actually paying for the drugs he'd gotten from them. From the day he came to Chill for work, he went on the list to be *"looked into."* That's a natural thing for the crew. It's true that the streets talk to them. But they have some law enforcement who worked for their forefathers too. Eddie failed that route miserably, so big Jake had Jake III and his boys to try the *drug buy angle.*

Big Jake decided to try for a smaller fish in the crew's pond. He knew Stoney stayed on a street which no other crew members lived on and the lived alone, for the most part. He was going for the shock and awe effect. He wanted to kill a crew member on Christmas. However he didn't know about the party Stoney was hosting that night.

Lil Jake's grandfather had promised him half of his estate if he could take down any member of the crew. Jake III did manage to kill Stoney but just like his father Jake Jr, he didn't live long enough to collect his reward.

Big Jake figured he'd better try the girl route after his grandson Jake III was killed. He had to see if he could break the crew males down by having 1 of their females to stray. Or better yet, become tainted because straying was the norm. He knew that was the 1 thing the males in the crew family, the strongest ones that is, took much pride in. A faithful woman who was submissive to him only. He wanted to change that, at all cost. After Eddie's mission failed, big Jake made going after Ebony his priority. That was when he made the statement about *showing her how to play.* But he didn't realize she was going back and forth to Houston. He thought he could get a boy to grab her attention because Ajay was still attending summer camps, back in 1989. Big Jake had preached about it

17

and kept it plastered all over his home, where it still remains. He had Craig and Carl to find some out-of-town guy who would come into their group. One who was handsome and athletic and would go after Ebony Brown with no fear of the crew, for he wouldn't know about them. Big Jake had this in the works for a few years. But he had focused in on Ajay from the time he was born. He had plans of knocking him off, long before his relationship with Ebony became news. Ajay was a basketball star by 7$^{th}$ grade, so he was in the news a lot. He was publicly dating Ebony by the 8$^{th}$ grade and he wasn't shy about letting it be known. Big Jake learned of it and started formulating a plot to ruin them immediately, years before Ajay was even old enough to go to college. That statement was made when Ajay was in 8$^{th}$ grade. Ajay and Ebony had become an item by then. The kids and the streets knew it because Ajay had staked his claim all over Abe Lincoln Middle school.

"You know the sixth grader, Ebony Brown?" he would say, "Well she's my woman. Don't say shit to her. If I hear about you fuckin wit her, in any way, I'm knockin yo fuckin head off. Is you ready for that? Cause I am."

That pretty much settled it. Ajay was known to beat the shit out of high school guys *and* fuck their girls before or shortly after. Most of the time, him fucking their girls was what had brought on the fight. He didn't give a damn about them or their girls. Neither of them was important to him.

He would say, "I don't want yo bitch, nigga. She came at me. She just wanted to give me the pussy, that's all. You're gonna keep her ass, though. And don't let her sweat me either."

Everybody already knew he was crew. He was popular, all the way around and never gave a fuck about it. He was real bold, ice cold and solid. A straight-to-the-point and never allowed things to linger, type of young man who didn't find time to

18

waste. He got to it and handled any bullshit, before it got legs. The girls were after him, not the other way around. With his outstanding ability and prolific talent, he was making the news every week. The size of his *"Johnson"* was getting street press daily, as well and that news spread just as fast. This was around the same time that the name Anthony "Ajay" Jackson became synonymous with basketball. Both in the state of Ohio and the United States. It's also when Mr. Bert Parkwood took public interest.

By word of Attorney George Wheeler, Bert Parkwood become something similar to a guardian angel for Ajay. He watched from afar, for years. But kept close contact with the crew family through their attorney. He was sent to Wheeler by the son of a man who was the same type of guardian for the crew, back in the days. Back when this whole beef with Jake Johnson got legs. Even though big Jake is yet to beat the crew, he'll never give up because he isn't the quitting type. Here is the real background into why this old man can't live out his life in peace.

Big Jake Johnson considered himself a crew enemy for decades. He's the age of the forefathers in Ajay's crew. He was also an enemy of one, Mr. Allen Saul Williams, mama Jo's deceased father. He became an enemy of Allen Devante' Jackson Sr, big Al's deceased father, simply because Al Sr wouldn't disown Allen Saul, take him under his wing and give him *"status."* Both men are Ajay's grandfathers and his legacies. Big Jake had vowed revenge on Allen Saul, back in the 50's. He took that beef up with the rest of his crew by the 60's. He has held this evil grudge since failing as a businessman in the 50's and 60's. He was in business with Allen Sr and Paul Sr, at the strip mall. He was an enemy of Allen Saul's simply because Allen Saul's wife, big Joanna wouldn't look his way.

19

But Allen Saul was fucking big Jake's women, on the regular. After Jake learned that Allen Saul had fucked the mother of his son, he tried hard to date Joanna Mae. That was before they had even bought a home in Cleveland. Allen Saul was fucking Jake's women while he was still in transit. He was yet to buy a Cleveland home and move his family. Though big Jake persisted, Joanna Mae wouldn't give him a glance. Joanna Mae told Allen Saul about big Jake's advances. That's when Allen Saul found big Jake and beat the crap out of him.

"That woman is mine, negro," Allen Saul said as he beat him. "Nobody fucks with my wife or my family. Or you best be expecting a beating. I fucked your girls. Yea I fucked em because they wanted me too. I just gave them what they asked me for and what they wanted."

Big Jake was thoroughly whooped and still he wouldn't leave well enough alone. He kept after Jo's mother and Allen Saul would whoop his ass. He would even send his son Jake Jr to school to bother Jo, Debbie and Richard. Allen Saul would beat his ass, worse. He had tried to infiltrate their crew and befriend other members. They were cordial to him, only because he hadn't become a threat yet. They even tried to help him become financially independent, thinking that would calm him down. But he thought he could wiggle his way into Allen Sr's good graces and become someone he would hold in higher regard then he did Allen Saul. That was impossible and Allen Sr made it known, at every turn. So after the business went south for big Jake. Plus a few other things which had failed for him, he took up that grudge he had for Jo's father and carried it over to big Al's father, Allen Devante' Jackson Sr.

Big Jake knew the crew was movement builders. He also should've known they wasn't going to carry him because they were loyal to Allen Saul. Big Jake was expected to pay his
20

own way, yet he failed too. Partially because he wasn't making the money they was making. And once he realized he wasn't a part of them, he took it very hard. That's when he started grooming his entire family to be opponents of the crew. It grew into a deadly and ugly situation, over the years. Simply because true love had overruled big Jake's ignorance, twice. Also because of his inability to be a strong and *real* head of household. He has held this grudge since the 1st generation was active because the crew are huge allies of equality and true love. Big Jake was always a yes man. He was okay with kissing a bigots ass and playing step and fetch it, just to try and gain acceptance. He also blames the crew for his only sister, Jessie Mae Johnson marrying Jeb Baker Jr. It was Allen Devante' Jackson Sr who introduced Jessie Mae to Jeb Jr, in 1950. Six years later, they had a daughter they named Rena Lynn Baker. But before any of this happened, there was a property deal which big Jake deemed inappropriate.

Jeb Baker Sr was the owner of the property where CrewLand mall is located today. After meeting Mr. Jeb Baker Sr and his son Jeb Jr, along the chitterling circuit, Allen Sr and Jeb Jr became fast friends. They all had a love of family and racial harmony. They also loved Jazz and Rhythm & Blues. The 3 of them would frequently hit up bars together in any town the tour stopped in. Often times these were type of bars that wouldn't have allowed Allen Sr in the door by himself. But the Baker's would get him in there, even if they had to pass him off as their driver.

"This here colored man is with us," Jeb Sr would say. Calling a black man, *a man,* in some places back in the day was enough to constitute a barroom brawl. But Jeb had power and lots of political juice. He could throw enough money around to
21

to calm even the staunchest redneck. Other times they would have to call in reinforcements which he always kept handy.

While in those juke joints, Allen Sr would sit proudly, shoulder to shoulder with the other white patrons. He became well known and relatively, well liked. Being a people's person is a Jackson male quality that became a noticeable genetic trait, especially by Ajay's generation.

During those late night juke sessions, Allen Sr discussed with the Bakers, his desire to own business property in Cleveland. He was planning to send his only daughter, Jessica, to Kent State when she became college age. He was looking for somewhere for her to make some money to get by on, while in college. He wanted this property to be something she could manage after she graduated. Jeb Sr told him about the very spot that is now the *CrewLand mall*. He told him it was for sale and he could buy it, for the right price. They eventually did the deal and the deed was transferred to Allen Sr. He owned it outright. But a black man owning commercial property in an influential zone of a lucrative city was something that was frowned upon, back in those days too. No matter how well off his family was, in *American* reality in those days, Allen Sr was still a black man. And he came from a very wealthy family who owned land in Boston. Owning property in Cleveland was a horse of a different color. But nevertheless, he owned it.

Jeb Jr was a good friend to Allen Sr. But his best friend and the reason he had come to the area, was named Paul Payne Sr, big Chill's grandfather. After Allen acquired the property, he added Paul Sr's name to the deed before any deal for repayment was ever even discussed. That's because they were like brothers, since neither of them had one. The deed read like Allen Sr owned it along with Paul Sr, from day one.

That went good, for more than a year. Then Paul Sr

22

introduced Allen Sr to Jacob Sr or big Jake. It wasn't long after, that all of their families met. Allen Saul and Joanna Mae knew of him because of their history. But they was back and forth, on the road, to the south during those days. Still registering voters, doing the political rallies and the protesting thing. Allen Sr and Paul Sr had discussed big Jake with Allen Saul and he gave them the history.

"He's a black man who needs some stability," Allen Saul said, "As long as he behaves himself and respects family values, then you can give him a little share. Just watch him and never give him enough for a controlling vote. Let him run his fruit stand, if he'd like. But he's not bringing in anyone."

"Solid," Allen Sr said and Paul Sr agreed.

Before this business venture, big Jake was a coworker of Paul Sr's at a refinery. The best job a black man could get in those days was maintenance. Paul Sr was the supervisor of the *"colored"* division. Big Jake owed him money. He had never tried to get out of paying him. Nor was he looking to be relocated. For that reason, Paul Sr figured they had no reason not to trust that he would work out. He just wasn't turning over money the way Paul Sr did. Not many did, for that matter. So to help big Jake have a bit more stability, Paul Sr suggested to Allen Sr that they give big Jake the opportunity to turn a buck. Allen Sr agreed, just on the word of his best friend and with the okay from Allen Saul. They cut Jake in as the minority owner and let him run 1 of the 8 suites.

Allen Sr had purchased the property from Jeb Baker Sr, in the late 40's. His plan was to do with it, exactly what the modern day crew have done. Set themselves up in business. Paul Sr and big Jake was from Cleveland and better known in the area then Allen Sr was, so he had offered them a share of
23

the property, in exchange for them helping him to maintain it and bring in local clientele. They all agreed. Then they worked out a payment plan which would enable Paul and big Jake to pay Allen Sr for their shares.

Paul Sr was a hustler. He could sell snow in Alaska, if that was all he had to work with. It took him very little time to get his money up. He had soon paid Allen Sr for his shares and became 50% owner, outright. Big Jake was good with his hands but he wasn't able to make money, the way Paul could. Allen's family had money already, so when he came to Cleveland from Boston, he was ready to buy and sale his way into another fortune.

In the meantime, big Jake's sister, Jessie Mae, had started a romance with Jeb Jr. This wasn't something her brother was in favor of. He was basing it strictly on race which was the same ignorance that many whites held toward their relationship. *No racial harmony allowed.* It simmered under the surface for a of couple years while Allen, Paul and big Jake tried to work together.

By 1952, there was 3 black men who was listed as prime real estate property owners in Cleveland Ohio. Shortly after, is when the bigoted sharks started to circle. It was during this same time that Jeb Jr and Jessie Mae's relationship was discovered by many whites, who didn't particularly favor the racial harmony, much like big Jake didn't. That fueled his insistence that his sister not date Jeb Jr.

"You gonna make these white folks kill all of us," big Jake would say, "They'll leave their own alone. But they'll damn sho kill you, me and our whole damn family."

The bigots started to make trouble for big Jake and in turn, that spelled the same trouble for Allen Sr and Paul Sr. But

24

Allen and Paul would buck against them and stand their ground. Not big Jake though. He would declare and make sure those bigots knew, he wasn't for the relationship either. He even went as far as making a deal with them to do away with his own sister. That was if they would only promise not to kill off his family. Allen Sr, Paul Sr and Allen Saul got wind of this declaration of big Jake's and from that day on, big Jake was ostracized. As long as he could pay his debt to them and his taxes, he could run his shop. But the crew wasn't willing to put any money behind him.

"Fuck his race trading ass," Paul Sr said.

"If the opportunity comes," Allen Sr said, "I'm gonna do his ass, myself. What a worthless piece of shit. He'll turn us over, first chance he gets."

The bigots put pressure on the city's leaders to unfairly tax the property or whatever they could do to make the crew men property ownership more of a hardship. In the 5 years since Allen Sr took possession, the cost of the taxes quadrupled from what they was when Jeb Sr was the owner. Still Allen Sr was able to keep up and Paul was just barely short, at times. Big Jake couldn't make his share of the bills, so Jeb Jr offered to pay it for him. Big Jake refused. Then Jeb Sr offered to secure a loan for him. Jake refused that also. He had asked Jeb Sr to hire him at the trucking company which would allow him to make up the difference. Or at least he could keep his head above water. Jeb Sr would've hired him but there was 1 problem. He had to have a drivers license to drive and a commercial license, to drive transfer trucks. Well Jake wasn't going to be able to drive the trucks because the city's leaders wouldn't allow him to pass the drivers test, simply because his black sister was in a relationship and about to marry, a white man. Big Jake blamed the Baker's and the crew for his sister

25

and Jeb Jr, ever meeting. Thus, he blamed them all for his racial troubles. As if the crew wasn't all living some part of it, themselves. It was many times that Allen Sr tried to reason this out with big Jake but he wanted to be stubborn about it.

"You set them up together," big Jake said, "And you're even friends with that Saul character too. He's always jumping me because his woman is sweet on me."
Jake was just delusional. He didn't want to make sense. And much like many of the crew enemies of the modern day, he just wanted to be a bitch. Jealousy and ignorance was the only reasons the crew could come up with to explain it.

"Either you pull your weight or you're gonna lose your spot," Allen Sr told him, "I came here to make something for the future of my family, my offspring and their offspring too. All you have is complaints. If you fuck with a man's wife a man's gonna whip your ass. That's a natural reflex. Instead of you looking for shit to lay on another brother, how about you stand as a damn man, yourself. I know you knew Paul from the plant and that's how you came in. But you will not be allowed to fuck up my business or my money. Is that understood? The only dependants I have is my wife Bertha and my two children. And when I bring them here to live, there won't be any stress and shit going on. Not any fuckin place where my wife is going to work, will there be any bullshit. So get your shit together now or get the fuck from round here."

"I need you to give me a loan," Jake tried, "I don't want no white man's money. He's trying to set me up."

"I'm going over here to get my house closed on," Allen Sr said, "Have a strategy when I get back or you're wolf food. I ain't got time for no hateful ass negroes, just like I ain't about to deal with no bigoted shit either."

Allen Sr had more pressing business to attend too. He

26

had to stop the eminent domain procedures that the city was putting forth to take his property. This is when Jeb Sr bought the property back and kept it in his name. He then willed it to Jeb Jr with the stipulation that it would belong, lock, stock and barrel, to Allen Sr and Paul Sr, upon his death.

Allen and Paul put the buy money into Savings Bonds. They said it would be for the benefit of their 1st born grandson's. Those grandson's would be born; Ajay and Chill. Jeb Jr was to oversea the property and see to it that it was put back in the rightful hands, if his father were to pass away. That is how the property was solidified and it would remain that way for a decade or more.

Big Jake had to take a buy out because he had fallen so far behind. He wasn't able to make the bare minimum he needed, through the business he ran there. Mainly because of the bigoted mobs. They would threaten and often times, attack folks who tried to patronize them and mostly him. Allen and the crew didn't mind fighting the bigots. So as cowards often do, the bigots would wield their greatest force toward the weaker one. That was big Jake. Still he would all but tap dance to win their approval and never got it. That just made Allen Sr livid.

In the meantime, the profits for the entire mall was cut drastically, on account of the angry mobs attacking the patrons. That's when Jeb Sr started to rent suites to whites, so they could make money off the place. That cooled down a lot of the tensions around there. Or at least it brought in some white business owners who now had something to lose. They soon put pressure on the city leaders to pass laws that would promote even more race relations in the city of Cleveland. Plus they was paying the rent. That was money which went directly to Allen Sr and Paul Sr. Jeb Baker was always saving the day for the

27

# MORE THAN 4 ADMIRERS-RELOADED

1$^{st}$ generation and that wasn't even the half of it. He did whatever was necessary for all involved to have harmony.

Big Jake's sister, Jessie Mae, had met Jeb Baker Jr in 1950. No matter how intense the firebombs and taunts got, they announced their engagement to both their families. They also voiced their desire to leave the country so they could live and love in peace. They were married by 1954. They moved to Europe, shortly after, with the help of Jeb Sr. Less than 2 years later, they had a daughter which they named Rena Lynn Baker. Allen Sr was asked to be her Godfather. Him and his wife, Bertha Lynn, flew to England to christen Rena. Rena was then given Bertha's middle name; Lynn. From that day on, they considered themselves blood. Rena and Allen Jr or big Al, would grow up as cousin's, though they wasn't blood related. Allen Sr and Bertha nicknamed her Josephine, after the great singer, Josephine Baker. But given an offspring the middle name of a close friend was something the 1st generation, of the crew, started. It became a family tradition and a sign of how dear the name lender was to the mother and father. It's an honor that's still prevalent with the modern day crew.

"She is so beautiful," Bertha said to Jessie Mae, "She could pass for white, you know."

"Half of her is," Jessie told her, "Now we'll see if there really is an advantage to this skin tone thing."

"Oh honey hush," Bertha said as they both laughed, "She's going to marry a future president."

"I want her to marry a black man, Bertha," Jessie said, "Jeb feels the same way. That's the only place he sees color. He wants his daughter to be treated like an equal in her home. And he sees a black man as being willing to do that, more so than the normal white man of today. They'll treat her like she's married to the house."

28

# MORE THAN 4 ADMIRERS-RELOADED

From then on, Jessie Mae was considered outcasts from the Johnson family. Her brother Jake cut all ties with her and said she had betrayed her family and her race.

Nevertheless, Jessie and Jeb Jr lived and loved from that day until the present. They had become so accustomed to racism, that once they was in Europe, they found themselves shunning others who didn't look or speak like them. That lasted only a short while. After all, they had a daughter who had to be schooled. For Rena Lynn, they bought a private school education. She was the sole grandchild and heir of the Jeb Baker Sr estate. The only conditions on the inheritance was that she had to live in America. Jeb Sr didn't like the fact that his only child had to move abroad. But at the same time, he understood the circumstances he was in and he wanted him to be safe.

The estate was Jeb Jr's to pass on to his daughter Rena. He did that but not until 1975. Jeb Sr passed away, 2 months after Rena Lynn married Archie Wilson, the son of Charles Wilson and 1 of Allen Sr's crew. By late 1976, they gave birth to a daughter whom they named Rebbie Shantell Wilson. She grew up as 1 of Ebony Brown's best friends. Or as big Jake called and still calls Ebony, *"the sheltered one."* Ebony and Rebbie grew up in the 3rd generation with Nina and T-baby. Collectively, they are known as; *The Awesome Foursome.*

Big Jake would wage war against Allen Sr and the entire crew, over what was ultimately his own short comings and ignorant hatred. There were many fights between the Johnson's and the crew. And many plays for the affections of the crew's women. None that ever netted any type of reward for big Jake or any of his allies, though they tried many times over the years.

29

Both Allen Sr and Paul Sr died, relatively young. However, they didn't die at the hands of big Jake. Allen Sr died of Prostate cancer in 1983, at the age of 62. Paul Sr died during the struggle in what was called a railroad accident. In truth, he died because of the way he demanded to live. With no obstructions between him and his pursuit of happiness. His death had everything to do with getting his freedom from Jim Crow, same as his good friend Allen Saul Williams. Paul Sr died in 1971. He did get to meet his 1st grandson, big Chill, before his passing. Allen Sr met his grandson Ajay, too.

## 2$^{nd}$ Generation

Big Jake had a son who was nearly the same age as the sons, Allen Sr and Paul Sr fathered. Allen Jr and Paul Jr were born in 1955. Jake Jr was born 2 years earlier in 1953. His father had raised him to hate the crew. While the crew men reared their sons without hate, they did give them the knowledge about their Johnson controversy. The females in the crew wasn't raised to know about this conflict because their men was going to keep the peace. The male folk in the Cleveland crew have to be aware of the vendetta big Jake has toward them. They are to be cognizant of it, whenever and wherever they roam. While big Jake was rearing his offspring to hate the crew, specifically. It didn't bring him many followers from his own era. The folks from the late 40's and on, admired the crew. The majority of Clevelanders looked for every opportunity they could to partner with the 1$^{st}$ generation because they admired their resolve.

The 2nd generation of the crew was a lot less patient with the Johnson bullshit than their fathers had been. Big Al, Paul Jr and the men in their crew, looked forward to it. Allen

30

# MORE THAN 4 ADMIRERS-RELOADED

Jr or bi Al came out to visit his sister Jessica, often. Every holiday and many weekends too. He was always trying to convince his dad to let him enroll in school there. Allen Sr allowed him to attend Cleveland schools by 1965. That was the icing on the cake for the still, very single Allen Devante' Jackson Jr. He was only 10 years old when he moved to Cleveland. He lived with his older sibling and sister, Jessica. She was 10 years older than him and attending Kent State. She was managing the strip mall but that part wasn't highly publicized. She had been in Cleveland since 1963. Her initial plans was to make Cleveland her home, after college and grad school. But all of that would change after she met Jonathan Layton.

Once big Al was in Cleveland, him, Paul Jr and big John Brown became like brothers. They hung together, dated together and they definitely fought together. There was always a fight to have, with big Jake constantly sending fools after them. Often times, they didn't wait for the fight to come to them. They went out to seek it.

By the late 60's, they stepped their game up to a street hustle and incorporated more guys, who was real men, like them. These guys were the sons of their fathers friends. The same type of men who prided themselves in being able to take care of their own. Big John, Brad, Sam and the others, along with Al and Paul, made quick waste of big Jake's excuses that he hated another man for not taking care of his *manly* duties, which were his alone. The 1st generation was known to handle big Jake's women, from time to time. Only because his women had come looking for *sexual healing*. The 2nd generation ran through them, as well. Big Al was sexually active when he moved to Cleveland. He was a ladies man and enjoyed women, twice his age. He had many of the girls who came to visit his

31

sister. They was attending college with Jessica and coming to the house, pretending they had to get study notes. When the only thing they was really studying was her brother. Big Al was a known stud who was oversized in his britches. That was what attracted the older girls. But he wasn't interested in staying with any of them. Not for long. Just long enough to get his thrills and move on. Most of them wasn't okay with that and wanted to bring trouble. But that wasn't going to be tolerated by Jessica. The older girls didn't wanting Jessica to know the depths of their anger. So they would back off and wait their turn to have whatever time Al was willing to share.

Knowing they was the 2$^{nd}$ generation of crew men to fuck the enemies women was a thrill for Al, John and their crew. They had fun with that bit of information. Big Jake and Jake Jr often found themselves ridiculed by many men during the late 60's and early 70's. And it wasn't only the crew that found them comical. Jake Jr and the crew squabbled a lot. Jacob Jr and his friends always lost those battles, just like his father's crew had. The 2$^{nd}$ generation was just as dominate as the 1$^{st}$, only a bit more lethal. They were partial to gun play and didn't hesitate to knock off an adversary. It was actually easier to do that, back then. A lot easier than it is for the modern day crew. Back then a black man missing wasn't even investigated thoroughly. The reason was usually the fear that it may turn out to be a white-on-black killing and they would have to try and find a way to sweep it under the rug. Anything to keep the Federal government from having to get involved. They didn't want to trade places with what Mississippi and Alabama was going through, at that time. From the Selma massacre to the 4 little black girls killed in the Birmingham church bombing, Alabama was making the news daily.
32

## MORE THAN 4 ADMIRERS-RELOADED

Not only them but the deaths of James Chaney, Andrew Goodman and Michael Schwerner, in Neshoba County, near Philadelphia Mississippi brought the Ku Klux Klan and Jim Crow laws to the attention of the world. So often when the crew would do away with 1 of big Jake's posse, they would go out and launch the search themselves. Then watch as law enforcement tried to bury it. That was very convenient for them. The 2nd generation of crew used that to their advantage. By the late 60's their family feud had started to rival *the Hatfield's and McCoy's*. It would prove to be just as deadly and span for many more generations.

Big Jake would out live his son, Jacob Jr and that was primarily his fault. He'd put his son in harms way with this idiotic rivalry he had started. Simply because of his economic failure. Or in laymen terms because another grown man wouldn't pay his bills for him. Jacob Jr did live long enough to make 2 sons before he was killed. One he named Albert and the other he named Jacob III.

Albert Johnson would have no parts of his family's rivalry. He was into peace and love. He loved to smoke weed. He grew up in the 80's. Smoking weed was a very popular pastime. After much pressure from his father and grandfather, to hate the east Cleveland crew, he grew tired of it. He eventually linked up with his aunt Jessie Mae and defected to Europe. Partly to escape being sucked into the rivalry with the crew and to avoid anymore senseless arguments with his ignorant father. The other reason was to avoid having to tell his family that he was gay. Other than his sexuality, Albert had many of the same beliefs as the crew. He saw no sense in living to kill them for thinking similar thoughts and acting on the same dislikes.

33

## MORE THAN 4 ADMIRERS-RELOADED

But Jacob III, who was 3 years his junior, bought into the beef hook, line and sinker. Primarily because he was given more praise for having a fight with a crew child, than he was for making good grades at school. Unfortunately his life didn't last as long as his father's did. Jake Jr was killed in 1985 just shy of his 32nd birthday. Jake III was gunned down 2 days into 1991 and hadn't quite reached the age to legally consume alcohol. However, he had killed the son of the guy who had gone to prison for killing his father. But in turn, his life was taken by the very crew that his grandfather and father had dedicated their lives to trying to destroy. *Here's that story.*

In 1967, a man who went by the name of Chester Lee was inducted into the crew which was later led by big John Brown. John became leader after Bradley Wilson was sent to the Vietnam war to avoid prison. Allen Jr wasn't the oldest and didn't feel he should be leader yet. Not before his brothers who was born there. He wouldn't be the head but he vowed to hold things down as the leader, whenever he was needed and better known in the area. Paul Jr and John had helped him to become familiar with the back streets and ally ways of Cleveland. It was only a matter of time before he knew the city like his birthplace of Boston Massachusetts and it was then that he solidified his crew stance. But Chester Lee was a Clevelander by birth, just as big Paul and John. They was all close with Bradley Wilson, Sam Logan and Brian James. It was a natural progression since all of their parents were close. By 1965, when Allen Saul was killed, the crew had brought all of the rest of the families together and to Cleveland. The families you will know, as the modern day crew. Though Allen Jackson Sr still wasn't calling Cleveland his official home yet, his daughter Jessica had been there since 1963 and his son Allen Jr had been enrolled in Cleveland schools.

34

## MORE THAN 4 ADMIRERS-RELOADED

Jessica lived in the house Allen Sr had purchased in what they now call, The Point. She was managing the strip mall for her father. The businesses had suffered over the previous decade. To make it less stressful on all involved, the heads of the families decided to rent out all 8 spaces and take regular jobs in factories, plants and schools. This was just until they could figure out a strategy to make the crew's businesses profitable again. Big John took a job with Jeb Baker's trucking company during his senior year of high school, in 1971.

But it was back in 1967 that Chester Lee was inducted, with his main goal being to kill himself a Jake. At the time he was initiated, he was shacking up with a lovely and flirtatious young sister named Jackie Coleman. He had met her through his friendship with Paul Jr or big Paul. Jackie was the best of friends with a *"taking-no-shit"* sister by the name of Willemena Wright. She was about to change her last name to Payne. Back then, Chill's mother and Stoney's mother was best buds and aces. Willemena introduced Jackie to Chester, just before he was initiated. They hit it off from day 1 and she moved in with him, after 3 months of dating. He owned a house on the corner of Union Ave and E. $72^{nd}$ street. Jackie wanted to get married but Chester wasn't convinced she was ready to be a wife and a family woman. She wanted to wear the pants and Chester wasn't going to have that. The 1 place they did agree with each other, on all cylinders, was in the bedroom. Their sex was awesome and all of their crew knew it. Because they always bragged about it. They very into each other, sexually. But once they left the bedroom, their relationship wasn't something that lifetimes was made of. They argued a lot and often times in public. The crew did their part and kept them focused and progressing.

By early 1969, Jackie and Willemena were with child.

35

## MORE THAN 4 ADMIRERS-RELOADED

But only Willemena's man, Paul Jr, had given her his last name. The fact that Chester was always saying he wasn't ready for marriage, kept the strain on him and Jackie's relationship. Still in all, both relationships bore sons. Willemena and Paul Jr's son Kenneth was born in June of 1969. They nicknamed him Chill, from day one. Jackie and Chester's son Cheston or Stoney, was born in October of 1969.

By 1970, the crew's 2nd generation was coming into it's own. There was several couples but only Paul Jr and Willamena had wed, so far. By the spring of the same year, at Kent State, Jessica was promoting a protest which was going to happen in May. Her and her brother Al was living in the home their father purchased. They was always having the biggest and best parties because their parents wasn't living there, year round. Al had many girls and all of them was older. But none of them he wanted for the long haul. Though he was a soldier and was very street wise, Jessica only saw him as her little brother. She was very protective of him, so when she was promoting the protest and he told her he wanted to be apart it, she tried to convince him not to join up. That didn't work. He signed up and recruited Paul Jr, John Brown and the rest of the crew. He loved the brotherhood they shared and he was surely ready to hold down his father's legacy with them. He loved Cleveland and the pack that his father had chosen to be apart of. He was going to see to it that it continued.

From the moment he 1st saw Paul and Chester's sons, he proclaimed them as the next generation. He was eager to have a son to partner with them but he still hadn't met the girl he wanted to call his own.

"They're gonna be the next generation of the crew," big Al said, "I'm gonna be here, so I've gotta find my misses, soon. Me and Jess got the house out by John's parents, so I'm in here

36

like I was born here. Just gotta find me a special girl I can hold, every night."

That was big Al, just before he met Joanna Lynn Williams better known as mama Jo. She was Allen Saul and Joanna Mae's daughter and oldest child. Big Al and mama Jo met at papa Brown and Granny Pearline's house on May 4, 1970.

Granny and her best friend Eloise Jones, who is better known as big mama and the rest of the mothers had made breakfast for all of the crew who was going to the protest at Kent State. Allen Saul's widow, Joanna Mae, was there with their 3 children; Joanna, Debbie and Richard. Joanna Lynn was fixing plates of food in the kitchen when big Al first spotted her. She glanced his way and their eyes locked. Suddenly, she turned away, too shy to look at him again. She smiled because his stare said something that sent chills through her. But once Al laid eyes on her, he couldn't stay in his seat. From the moment he saw Jo, his eyes didn't leave her. He got up from his chair and went to her, immediately. Jo was in the kitchen with Pearl, whom Al knew already as John's girl. They was helping their mothers fix plates for all of the crew, so everyone could have breakfast together. Men folk wasn't allowed in the kitchen, back then. And not too much now. They saved their cooking for the grills. But Al had to get in there and find out who this beauty was.

Jo had very smooth, butter cream colored skin. Her hair was jet black, shiny and hung down her back, nearly touching the arch above her buttocks. She had strong native American features like a modern day Pocahontas. He wanted to see her beautiful brown eyes again, so he stepped across the threshold which separated the parlor from the kitchen.

"Hey," he said as he walked up to her.

Mother's Annabelle and Sally was protesting a boy being in

37

the ladies kitchen but Al was on a mission. Big mama told Sally and Annabelle to let him be.

"He's sweet on Joanna's girl," big mama had said, "He's got her father's name. Allen Saul would've hand picked Allen Sr's boy for his daughter, if he was still alive. Let them meet. She's just shy of seventeen. It's time for her meet her a husband."

With that, Sally and Annabelle backed off while Granny and big mama coaxed Jo to answer Al back. He didn't know how long it would take to get her to his table. But he was willing to risk being fussed at, if it meant getting her name and getting her to sit with him, so he could find out how to find her later. Jo looked at him, shyly. She had smiled at him brightly when he spoke to her. But she wouldn't let her eyes stay fixed on his, for very long. That made him want her attention all the more. She finally spoke.

"Hi," she said, "Do you want me to make you a plate?" she asked and she smiled again.

He knew she was attracted to him, from that moment. Because she couldn't look at him for very long without blushing.

"Sure," he said, "But only if you'll bring your plate and eat at my table."

"Okay," she said, "You're sitting with John. That's my best friends boyfriend. She was going to introduce me to you when we got done in here."

She accepted his invitation. She joined him, John and Pearl, for breakfast. From that point on, they have hardly left each others side.

"Al, this is Joanna," John said as they all sat down to eat, "Her daddy and your daddy was aces. I wanted you to meet her. She's single too. She lives out by Paul and Willa, like right across the street."

38

"She's my best friend," Pearl adds, "And she's starting to feel like a big sister to me and my little sister, Brenda. Her parents are in our parents crew. She's an activist, just like you are, Al. Her father was killed in Birmingham on a freedom ride."

"Okay Pearl, thanks," John says, "But he's gonna think Jo can't talk, in a minute."

They all laugh. Al was already impressed with her legacy and equally impressed by her beauty and manners. He could tell she was a virtuous girl, just by the way she was seated at the table and by the way she spoke. He was so eager to hear her speak again and if he could, he was going to make sure she was talking, only to him. He continued to stare at Jo, even while Pearl and John was speaking. Jo was taken by him, instantly. They all noticed that. She decided to invite him to spend the day with her because she didn't want the meeting to end either.

"So are you going to the protest?" she asked him.

"Oh for sure," he says, "Activism is my passion. But I'm sure this one is going to turn into a life changer for me."

"For me too," Jo said.

"We already have something in common," he said. Then he asked with a huge smile, "I'm going to go on and asked you now, so I can get this outta the way and done. Will you have the rest of your meals with me? I wanna know if you'll be my girlfriend?"

He was still smiling when he asked her that. She felt so shy, all of sudden. It was definitely something special about this man.

Joanna Lynn Williams was hardly ever at a lose for words. But it was apparent to everyone around them that Al had her shook. She was known to be a very outspoken sister. She spoke at rallies and protest, all the time. Even more in the last 5 years, since her father was killed. She had taken up his

39

tenacity and kept it going. But around big Al, she felt suddenly shy. She didn't know how to answer him without smiling. Probably because he kept smiling at her and looking directly into her eyes.

He was a gorgeous brother. He had the smoothest black skin she'd ever seen and his conversation was smooth, as well. She could tell he was very confident. He wasn't the arrogant type, by any means. But he wasn't shy about saying what he felt. That was the part she loved, the most. He had only known her for about 15 minutes and he was already cautioning others about what they could and could not say to her. And how he wanted her treated from that day forward.

"So are you gonna answer me?" he asked as he flashed her a picture perfect smile.

He had pearly white teeth and they was well cared for. His lips were smooth and dark by nature. She could tell he smoked but he didn't smell of cigarettes. His eyes were black and they seemed to sparkle when he smiled. His stare was sharp and to her, he seemed to know she found it hard to stare back at him. That didn't stop him from staring at her, the entire breakfast, though. He was very tall, very dark and very handsome. All 3 of those were things she liked in a boy. He was like an Otis Redding but taller. After only a brief conversation, he had already discovered she was 1 and a half years his senior. That turned him on.

"So I guess my wife is going to be older than me," he said and smiled, "But I'll be the man of my house. Allen is always the man."

"That was my father's name," Jo told him, "He was killed on the first day of this month, five years ago."

"I hope that's a sign that he's in favor of me," Al says, "He was a great man. He visited our home in Boston, many

40

times. Him and my father was tight like brothers. I just never knew he had a daughter so breathtaking."

"I think you're very handsome," she says, "And very charming too."

From that morning to the present, they were an official couple. Al had found the woman he wanted to marry and have babies with.

They would court for 2 years and 11 days. They became the 3$^{rd}$ couple in their crew to get engaged, though many were dating long before them. Al didn't believe in wasting time. When he made up his mind about something, he got it done.

On the 15$^{th}$ day of May in 1972, they were married. Less than a year later, they started their family. Their oldest child, a girl they named Lynora, was born in early April of 1973. They called her Lynn after Al's mother, Bertha Lynn. They birthed 1 son which Al named Anthony. Al and Jo call him Ant while most everyone else calls him, Ajay. He was the spitting image of his daddy and his daddy's daddy. Jo and Al had decided not to name him Allen because there were already 3 of them.

"We're going to let him start his own legacy," Al said and Jo agreed.

"I want him to be just like you, Allen," Jo said.

"He won't have a choice," Al answered and they laughed.

They had a total of 5 children and Ajay was their only son.

By 1975, the 2$^{nd}$ generation of the crew was all married, all except Chester and Jackie. After all this time they, still hadn't married. Jackie was still after him about it and he was still stalling but their sex life never faltered or tapered off. They had a baby girl in 1981 and another girl by 1984. The 3$^{rd}$ generation of the crew was already forming by their 3$^{rd}$ child's

41

birth but the 2$^{nd}$ generation still had some unfinished business with big Jake. They remained active, well into parenthood.

One Thursday night in 1985 while Al, John, and big Richard was hanging out in Brook Park, a gang of more than 20 men jumped them. They beat them, pretty badly and left them for dead. Those 20 guys were sent by big Jake. No one even had to question that but if they had any questions, they were quickly answered when big Jake claimed the deed before it had time to make the news. To add insult to injury, big Jake had parties planned all over the west side of Cleveland, starting from Lorain avenue all the way to the town of Lorain. However, when Paul, Chester and the 2$^{nd}$ generation of males got wind of it, an all out war was called and waged against big Jake. No matter where they saw them or anyone representing them, they were ordered dead on the spot.

Big John and Pearl had a hot evening planned for that Friday. But after he was beaten up, John didn't want to get laid. All he wanted to do was get even.

"Baby, I don't think you should go out again tonight," Pearl said, "You haven't healed up. I think you should give yourself time to heal."

"Pearlie, I'll never heal sitting around this damn house," he said, "I'm gonna stomp the shit out them negroes tonight. One by one, if I have too. That sneak attack shit gets no play with the crew. They're gonna have to stand as men, one damn day. May as well start today."

"But what happened to my lover man?" she asked, hoping her desires would win out over a street brawl.
But big John had his mind set for war. He knew things would be way to rough for her, in the bedroom, if he was to go in on
42

her while trying to suppress his temper. With all of the pinned up aggression he was holding, sex for her would feel like an assault.

"I'll love you down when I get back here, baby," he said, "I got business to tend too. You know your man."

"I need you to be sure and get back here too, John," she stressed, "Please. Promise me you'll-"

"Baby, I'm coming home," he said, "I'm just gonna make sure that a few of their asses *don't* make it home."

With that, he grabbed his tools and headed down the stairs to where their 4 children was waiting at the bottom.

"Daddy can I go with you," his only daughter Ebony asked.

She had tears in her eyes. She was afraid. She had listened to her father rant and rave, all day, with his temper on maximum. The plan his crew had set wasn't to unfold until tonight. It took everything his crew brothers had and even Pearl to, to keep John from taking off on his own.

"No baby girl," he said, "Daddy can't take you on this run. I'll take you to the store tomorrow and buy you a pretty dress. Both you and your mama, okay?"

"Okay daddy," 9 year old Ebony answered, "You promise?"

"I promise, sweetheart," John said as he prepared to leave.

12 year old John Jr, whom they call Jb and 10 year old son, Jeremy, whom everyone calls Tank, was going with him. It wasn't the 1st trip for either of them. The boys going was what made Ebony want to go, all the more. But she wasn't going. This was a male thing. *Period.*

She followed them as far as the door. Her, Pearl and 4 year-old Jesse stood in the doorway. John, Jb and Tank went

43

on out and met up with Al and his 11 year-old son Ajay, near the front of Al and Jo's new van. Ajay made eye contact with Ebony as she stood watching. He likes her. She knows it now. They've kissed once, lips to lips. He's taking it very slow with her, now that she speaks to him, all the time. She didn't use too. She use to act afraid of him and that bothered him, more than any other thing did. For all he wanted to do was protect her from any harm. He smiles at her. She smiles back. She can see a bulge at his waist. It's a 357 magnum but she doesn't know. It's the 1 his grandpa Allen Sr had left for him. Richard Sr was pulling into the driveway. Paul Jr was coming from his house across the street. His son, 16 year-old Kenneth, nickname Chill, was with him. He's the head of the 3$^{rd}$ generation and he was expected to have the strategy for his crew. He did. Chill was Paul Jr and Willamena's only child. He has a son, who is his namesake. Kenneth Jr is nearly 2 years old. He has a Christmas birthday, just like Ebony does. Kenneth and his mother Renee, are going to wait at Jo and Al's house until the men return.

The ladies in the crew know some danger is out there. Because their men have told them all to watch each other and stay on their blocks until they tell them different. These men and their sons are about to put on a full court press. It's about time big Jake felt the wrath of this crew. This is something they have to do, about every 2 to 5 years, just to make sure big Jake doesn't forget the crew will remove any and all stumbling blocks, whenever and by any means necessary.

On this particular night, big John, Al and big Paul, along with Chester, Richard and John's younger brother Greg, set a trap at a pub called, *The Landmark*. It was on the corner of Brook Park road and W. 150$^{th}$ street. They leaked and let

44

the word get out, that only John, Al and Richard was in there alone, again tonight. This time the word was that they was feeling up some honeys and drinking heavily. When in fact, they were all laying in wait, above that point. Just off of the corner of Rocky River road. They was waiting for big Jake's boys to come through celebrating, while on the way to what they thought would be an ambush or a surprise attack.

"I'm bussin these fuckers up like watermelons, as soon as I see one," Chester Lee said, "I'm bout sick of these dumb ass bitches, anyway."

Chill had Ajay and Tank loading extra clips while him and Jb waited next to a large oak tree and a staged vehicle, on the side of the road. They were going to throw out homemade tire spikes to disable the vehicles as they passed. They was about 20 yards up the road from where their fathers was, so by the time the tires deflated, the cars would come to a stop right in front of where the fathers where staged. And they was going to open up on them. The grandfathers who had come along, were even farther down the road. Just in case any of the guys got through the crew's road block. The majority of the grandfathers stayed behind to guard the women, the children and the homes.

The ambush happened just as they had planned it. Big Jake's guys was caught off guard when the tires on the vehicles that was headed to The Landmark, blew out under them. There were other cars too. But once they saw what was happening to the cars in front, they retreated as Ajay and Tank fired upon them with fully automatic weapons. John and the guys beat some and shot others, until no one was left moving. 8 of big Jakes guys perished that night. Amongst those killed was Jake Johnson Jr. Big Jake's only son. Instead of big Jake ending the war which costs him his son. He stepped it into overdrive. He vowed to take the sons of the men who had killed

45

his son. He started out with sending the police to Shaker Heights. He stated John, Al and Paul had killed his son. That was a fact but there was no proof.

"That is one bitch ass negro," big Al had said.

"No shit, man," John agreed, "He talked all that shit about how he was sending his son to whip our asses again."

"Then his shit fails," Richard said, "Like it always do."

"And that's when he wants to bitch and moan," Paul added.

"Wheeler's on it," papa Brown told them.

Introducing, young George Wheeler, an attorney who had come on as the families counsel in the early 1970's. He had been handpicked by Jeb Baker Sr before he passed away. Wheeler had attended school with Jeb Jr, who still resides in Europe with his wife, Jessie Mae. Through Wheeler, all crew legal woes would be handled, as well as any estate matters. For political power, Jeb Jr had forwarded information to Wheeler about his Alumni, Bert Parkwood of the University of Cincinnati. Parkwood was a political wiz and reminded Jeb of his father, the late Jeb Sr. With Wheeler and Parkwood as the crew's legal bodyguards and guidance team, there wasn't any legal battle they wouldn't be prepared to face. And they would have one of their toughest battles within the next year.

In mid 1986, the trial for the massacre was set. John, Al, Paul, Sam and Richard was all implicated and facing prison time. But not 1 of them got any serious time. Basically, they got time served or community service. Most had served anywhere for 4 days to 2 months behind bars, between the week after the massacre and May 1986. But there was no way to know who had actually done the murders. The crew was just that good.

46

They hadn't left any evidence. Thing is, it was done so professionally that law enforcement didn't even believe they were capable of it. But they were.

To avoid a lengthy trial and also to get out of having to face time for drug possession, Chester Lee copped to the murder of Jacob Johnson Jr, only. He received a life sentence. He took 1 for the crew, is what he'd done. Because Al and John had killed Jake Jr with their bare hands. Chester wasn't even close to him. Since Chester and Richard was the only crew with any type of criminal record and to save the justice system from dismantling the families, they took the rap. Richard went to jail for damage to vehicles. Chester pled guilty to murdering Jake Jr, even though he hadn't even been implicated. Once that was over, rather then big Jake being satisfied that someone was locked doing time for his son's murder, he held on to his vow to delete the crew. He still held his vendetta against both Allen's and he wasn't letting it go. Chester was sentenced to federal time and sent to California to serve.

Several months later, Jackie Coleman moved to Columbus Ohio and took their 2 daughters. Stoney wasn't going to leave Cleveland nor his crew. The crew had vowed to take care of Chester's family but initially, Jackie held a grudge. Not because Chester went to prison, for she was none the wiser that he hadn't done it. She thought he had because he'd killed before. What she was angry about was, he never married her. She met a Caucasian man named Jason Carr and followed him to Columbus. The crew didn't have a problem with him. They wanted him and Jackie to stay in Cleveland and remain crew. But Jackie said she needed a break.

"It's too much damn death and destruction going on around here," she had said, "I need to get my girls out of here until this beef shit cools down. Stoney don't wanna leave. He'll

47

be seventeen, next month. He wants to stay here with Chill and his crew. I understand that. I would never separate him from the only brothers he knows. He can have the house. I can't do this right now."

That was September 1987. She moved just after Christmas, of the same year. Stoney was killed 3 years later as a result of the beef his mother Jackie had run from.

In the middle of January of 1988, while they rode home from their legal jobs. Brian, Sam, Archie, Brad and Paul's vehicle was shot up. The vehicle was riddled with bullet holes and ruled as an act of gang violence. Every brother in that van was shot. Some worse than others but none more serious than Paul Jr. He was shot in the head and taken to East General for immediate surgery. He wasn't given a chance to make it but the crew had held onto hope. He was the last blood family big Chill had left. He survived the operation and then some. Unfortunately, he would succumb to his injuries 2 weeks later, on January 31, 1988. That was the last day big Chill gave a fuck about making peace with anybody, let alone ending the war with the Johnson's. He had registered to vote, just 7 months prior. Voting was something his grandmother and his mother always told him he had to do as soon as he turned 18 years old. Well, he had. Now he was without his grandparents and his parents at 18 years of age. His son had just turned 4 years old. His girlfriend of 6 years, Renee Stewart was in need of a permanent home because her mother had disclaimed her, right after their son was born. Big Chill changed Renee's legal address to his home in Shaker Heights and she became lead female of the crew's 3rd generation.

This war was something that started years before this 3rd generation was formed or before they were even born. The 48 desire to rid the crew of their power has been in big Jake and several of his family members minds. They wanted the power and the love the crew had and they wanted the finances and leadership too. But from big Jake on down, they was to stubborn and outright stupid to even ask for it. When it came to hand outs, big Jake already knew he wasn't going to get one from anyone in the Cleveland crew.

For this reason, the crews history is always considered whenever they make any move. The ladies don't know the particulars but as they become older, they learn more about the Johnson's and the family beef. But the war doesn't end for big Jake. He just finds a new route and presses on. It won't end until he dies. That's something the 3$^{rd}$ generation of males are determined to see too. Stoney and Chill had discussed it often, along with Rob Jenkins, who was their age also. They resolved, some years ago, that big Jake will be a star in their generations crown. Rob's biological father had been killed during this beef and he wasn't even crew. He was just partial to them.

With a bit more of the history given, let's go back to June of 1989 through Christmas season of 1990.

Sending Eddie to infiltrate and pretend to be a drug dealer didn't work for a few reasons. He was trying to string Ajay out, at the worst time. An attempt on Ajay in 1989 was harder than it would've been on any other crew member. Ajay was still attending those exclusive summer camps. Plus Bert Parkwood had so much press and influential people around him when he was in public that none of big Jake's guys could even get close. Parkwood had counted on that. Besides Eddie's real intent was known, not long after he had surfaced.

The Ebony plan had been foiled because she moved to Houston. Big Jake knew poppa Jones had the whole Houston

49

police department behind him, to a certain extent, so they went back, regrouped and came up with Stoney. The youngest Jake wanted to do Stoney because he knew Stoney's father was in prison for killing his father. Jake III wanted to kill Stoney, first and they had a plan. But the first plan was scrapped because Stoney went to county jail for assault in early 1989. He had beat the hell out of a boy who slapped his girlfriend Breanna, out at Gordon Park, one December evening. The young man's family had pressed charges and Breanna's family didn't. They wanted Chill and the crew to handle him in their own way. After Stoney went to jail on the charges, the crew decided to lay off and let the heat die down. They would get him later. Ajay didn't lay low. He went and killed him, solo. Breanna is his 1st cousin, by blood.

Young Jake was 1 of the murderers of crew member Stoney Coleman. That came about after several other plans had to be scrapped. The first scenario was hatched in 1988, right after word got out that Jackie Coleman was moving to Columbus. That plan didn't work out, so they came back to it in 1990.

"I have to kill that bitch ass nigga," young Jake had said, "His father killed my daddy, then that nigga ran off to the feds so he couldn't be touched."

"Well we gonna touch his seed," Greg Harrison had said, "That nigga live by himself. We already staked out the crib. We can move on his ass during the holidays. Danny got some news too."

"What you got, Danny?" young Jake had asked.

"I got a cousin who's gonna be going to Cleveland State," Danny Washington said. "His name is Justin. Justin Warner. His pops is Jewish but his mom is my auntie. He down

50

to do some bangin for this blood. He already told me he's in."

"Let's go to my granddads house," Jake III had told them, "We need to bring him up on what we got and see what else he wanna add to it."

They went to see big Jake. It was then that Carl and Craig was brought into the fray, along with Justin and Tim.

Big Jake told them he wanted them to go after the foursome girls, namely Ebony Brown. That night they came up with the plan to go after the foursome, in an attempt to get to Ebony and spoil her. They had no idea she was going to be living in Houston. After not being able to get Ajay, Ebony nor Chill in 1990, that was the reason they went back to their initial plan to get Stoney.

Greg Harrison, Justin and Tim had passed by Ebony's house, several times during the 1990 Christmas season. They saw she was home but they had no clue about the particulars because the streets were loyal to the crew. They had come through early Christmas morning.

"Is these motherfuckahz having a snowball *fight*?" Greg had asked while Tim and Justin cracked up laughing.

"Oh that's real gangster," Tim said sarcastically.
But when they reported back to big Jake, he told them to take their time getting to Ebony because she was always going to be surrounded.

"We can wait on that until Ajay goes to college, if we have too," big Jake told them, "Because if he's anything like his grandfather, he's not gonna let her out of his sight, as long as he's around."

"They be handcuffing they ho's," Jake III said, "While at the same time, they fuckin wit all of ours."

"We'll fix all that shit for Christmas," Danny had said, "We're gonna be Santa Claus to that nigga, Stoney."

51

# MORE THAN 4 ADMIRERS-RELOADED

The next day, Greg, Jake III and Danny laid in wait for Stoney. It was early on Christmas evening when they started to creep around Union Avenue, waiting for Stoney to show up. But when Stoney came home from dinner with his crew, he had Jb, Lynn, Rob, Jan and Bre with him. They was getting ready to set up for the Christmas party, Stoney was hosting.

"This nigga came home with company," Jake III said.

"We'll chill down the block and watch the house," Greg said, "Pull down by seventy fifth. We'll chill in the cut, by that impound lot. Then we'll go back when it's clear."

"One of them ho's that just went inside with him was Ajay's sister," Jake III told them.

"Yep," Greg said, "That's that track star, bitch. She probably packing too."

They all laughed but they didn't underestimate either of the 6 crew members who had just entered Stoney's house. They preferred to try and catch Stoney alone.

"Let's do the buy plan first," Danny suggested, "That way we can see what he's got up and how long he's gonna have all them other bitches around there."

Stoney and the crew had gone inside to get things prepared for the party and to get dressed.

About 30 minutes later, Jake III, Greg and Danny pulled back up to the house, parked and tooted the horn. Stoney came out to the car while Jb and Rob waited on the porch. The crew never figured the guys was brazen enough to try to hit them in their neighborhood but there would be a lesson learned within the next 24 hours.

"Stoney what you got up?" Danny asked while Jake sat quietly in the backseat.

"What you need?" Stoney had asked, not willing to have idle conversation with any of them.

52

Him, just like his crew, knew about the beef the crew had with the Johnson's but this was the dope game. Rules are a little different. Enemies are willing to cross lines to get their product cheaper, so that's the route these enemies was trying, this evening. But Stoney wasn't divulging any information about his plans.

He told them, "Let me know what you wanna cop. Let's do this, so you can move on."

They started to haggle and tried to stall for time. That is until they saw Chill's Blazer pull up. Chill hopped out quickly and came directly to the other side of their car. Rob trotted out and stood in front while Jb moved over and hovered near the back of the black and white sedan. Once the 3 guys saw the stance the crew had taken, they knew they would die on the spot if they acted out aggressively. Chill was looking directly at Greg Harrison and hoping he flinched wrong or acted as if he was reaching under his seat. Rob had Danny, who was the driver while Jb checked Jake in the backseat.

"What you need, nigga," Stoney pressed, "Hurry this shit up!"

"You only gonna get what you can pay for," Chill added, "So make a move, like my partner said, so y'all can get the hell on."

With that, he sped the deal up and sent them on their way. He took Stoney, Jb and Rob off to the side and reminded them not to trust the Johnson's.

"Look y'all know what the father's told us and what we already know about that Johnson click," Chill said, "Never approach them *niggaz* alone. Just me seeing them show up here, tells me they on some dumb shit. Stoney you needs to double up tonight. Keep some crew handy."

Stoney said, "Them coward ass niggaz ain't gone buss a grape in a fruit fight. You saw the fear in their faces?"

53

"Not with all of us here," Chill told him, "But we ain't gonna play them low. I want them niggaz to know they on front street."

"They after you and Ajay, mainly," Rob says, "And we ain't gonna take none of that shit lightly. So while y'all party, me, junior and Jb is about to roll to the motel and sit out. While Ajay and baby girl up in there. We got that assignment tonight."

"Cool," Chill said.

Him and Stoney went inside to officially kick off the party while Jb, Rob and Jr headed to the motel. They were going to lay in the cut. The crew was thinking the reason Jake and his boys was on the eastside was because they were planning to ambush Ajay at the motel. When in reality, they were going for Stoney, all along.

Jake, Danny and Greg rode off and down Union Avenue. They turned north on east 131$^{st}$ street and headed to Shaker Boulevard. From Shaker, they headed east to Lee road and rode passed the library. They drove south to highway 480 and from there, they went west to I-77. Then north to the Cleveland Lakefront. They knew they would have a long wait before the crew would clear out and they wasn't going to risk trying to wait anywhere on the eastside.

"I was gonna say we could go by Jade's spot, over at the University apartments," Greg said, "But now that I know them crew niggaz got a party, that means some of them niggaz might be out that way before we can get out of there."

"Hell yea," Jake says, "Probably fuckin somebody's bitch while that nigga at they party."

"Them some low down motherfuckahz, homie," Danny added as they pass by CSU, hopped on alternative highway 6 and made their way to the lakefront parking.

54

## MORE THAN 4 ADMIRERS-RELOADED

They was going to grab a burger and hang out there. Then go back to Stoney's house before daylight.

Meanwhile, while Rob, Jb and Jr sat on guard outside, Ajay and Ebony enjoyed each others company in room 111. It was their 2nd time in that same room.

"Has this been a good birthday for you, baby girl?" Ajay asked Ebony while he kissed her face and played with her nipples.

"Yes," she said, "It started when I saw you stay back at mama Jo's house, this morning. That made me smile."

"Yea she aw ight," he joked and they both laughed.

Ajay hadn't stayed at his mothers house for weeks. That was something the Cleveland guys was more worried about than they had let on to Ebony and the girls. But for the past 5 weeks, Chill and the guys had been guarding spots were Ajay would be without even telling him they were doing so. Ajay was always so independent minded and he never had much patience for doing anything he wasn't interested in or willing to do. He stayed at an apartment in Maple Heights with an older woman named Darlene Casey. That move happened 1 afternoon before Thanksgiving, after him and his mother Jo had a full blown argument. His father didn't like that he left. But he knew he would be watching his every move, along with his crew brothers. And at the same time, he would convince Chill to find a way to get Ajay to stay at his home, instead of Maple Heights. As it turned out, Ebony was the person who convinced him to move back to Shaker Heights and she didn't even have to ask him too.

"Do you like how sex feels yet?" Ajay asked as they laid in each others arms.

"Most of it," she answered with a smile.

55

"What do you mean, most of it?" he asked smiling back at her but really wanting to know her answer.

"You get carried away after you give me that good feeling," she answered slowly and shyly.

"That's an orgasm, Ebony," He had told her, "You are *so shy* about talking sex."

He chuckled and asked, "Why is that? Cause I know that's all you and your girls talk about."

"I don't know but that's not all we talk about," she corrected him, "We talk about our family stuff too. Like how different it is for the guys, then it is for us. And how y'all can hang out with the fathers and grandfathers and it's never any pressure. Y'all talk about the same things with daddy's crew as y'all do with each other."

"It's a crew thing," he said and chuckled. He had to steer her from that conversation, so he said, "Say orgasm."

She giggled. He just stared at her. He was waiting for her to do what he had told her to do which was to answer him. She stalled because she was very shy about talking openly to him about sex.

"Say it baby," he demanded.

"Orgasm."

"Was that hard?" he asked.

"Sort of, yes," she said.

He smiled as he started to kiss her again. He was in the mood and very turned on, just by the way he could get her to submit to him. He pulled her closer, took her hand and placed it on his dick.

With a devilish smile he said, "Not as hard as this."

He mounted her again and they made love, a $2^{nd}$ time.

It was late when the party ended. Ebony, Ajay and the guys had made it back about 1am. They partied for 3 more
56

hours before the time came to shut it down and go home. Chill and Jr had given engagement rings to their girls and they all celebrated the 1st engagements of their crew. They had no idea that 1 of them wouldn't be apart of the next party.

But by 8am the same morning, Stoney was dead and the crew were distraught. This was the 1st death for this 3rd generation. All of the males knew what this was about and they wanted closure, immediately. It didn't take long for them to piece together the suspect list either. They knew Lil Jake already. They had to find out the names of the other 2 who was in that Black and White Impala with him, the night before. They found out the drivers name, on the same day. They also found out he was Eddie's brother. His name was Danny Washington and he was in a coma at West General, out in Westlake. They knew Stoney had gotten 1 of the guys who killed him. They also knew that was Stoney's way of leaving them a clue. Danny Washington would be laid up for along while. He wouldn't be going anywhere, anytime soon. They put a tab on him so they would be informed of when he was released and where he would be staying. They was going to go and kill him after he got home and not even allow him to fully recover.

But first, they had to bury their crew member and brother. Brad Sr, who was Bre and Jr's father, sent a kite to the federal prison in California. He informed Chester Lee that his son had been killed. He would find out later when his daughter Bre visited him, that Chester never received it.

The day after Stoney's service, the crew got not only the name of the 3$^{rd}$ guy, Greg Harrison. But they found out him and Jake's whereabouts too. With the help of the streets and a CSU brother and crew member, Arthur Owens, they knew exactly where to find all 3 of big Jakes employees, who'd taken

57

the life of their crew brother. It was exactly 1 week to the day that Stoney was pronounced dead, when Chill, Ajay, Tank, Rob, Jb and Jr rolled on Jake and Greg. They were shoveling snow from around their getaway car, at the University apartments. They killed them with ease and left no traces. There was no trial and if there was an investigation, it never came toward the crew. The police was looking for gang members and the crew moved on from there.

Later they found out Stoney's girlfriend and crew member, Breanna or Bre as they call her, was pregnant. She would give birth to a baby girl in 1991, that she named Chastity Jaquel Coleman. Not long after the birth, Jackie Coleman moved back to the old neighborhood with her entire family.

When Lil Jake was murdered, many thought that was the end of the threat to the crew. They knew big Jake didn't have anymore sons or grandsons in the Cleveland area. Albert was in touch with the crew more than he was his grandpa Jake, so the crew knew his mind hadn't changed. But it soon became clear that it wasn't the end. Big Jake had a few more angles to try on the 3$^{rd}$ generation.

Summer 1992, after Ajay graduated high school and was preparing for his 1st year of college at the University of Cincinnati, big Jake had regrouped and unleashed a new plan. It was June, 2 Saturdays before fathers day and the foursome, which consisted of Ebony, Rebbie, Nina and T-baby, was going to *Richmond Town Square mall* to shop and hang out. That's when into the lives of this crew, came 4 guys who made claims of being smitten by the foursome girls. In reality, their plan was to infiltrate the crew through these young ladies. Then slowly tear down and destroy them. That was big Jake's latest plan. He thought this would surely work because none of the
58

guys had his last name. One of them wasn't even from Cleveland and the other 3 was from Bedford Heights, by way of Akron and Youngstown. Big Jake felt he would have another win and he was counting on this 1 being significant. He knew the only way to make a real mark on Ajay was to get Ebony.

The foursome arrived at the mall, ordered a slice and a garden salad combo, then they grabbed a booth just in front of *Sbarro's Pizza*. Before they could sit down and get comfortable, T-baby noticed 4 healthy young men staring at them, as they walked into the same mall entrance the girls had just come through. T-baby commented to her girls that the guys was staring, smiling and approaching, while Ebony discouraged her from looking their way. She didn't listen. To others it may look like they planned to meet there, the way the 4 guys made a beeline toward them. They stepped to the foursome with the full intent of sabotaging all 4 of them. But Ebony Brown was their ultimate target. This was also during the time when Nina, T-baby and Rebbie was claiming their independence from Tank, Rich and June, because of their cheating ways. Ebony had never made such a claim nor was she planning too. Ajay wouldn't have allowed it anyway. He was never going to be broken up with her. However, the girls had refused to shop for Ajay's new apartment and had communicated that to Tank.

When the 4 guys approached their booth, all Nina and T-baby saw was admirers. Rebbie saw 4 guys whom she thought liked them but she knew she wasn't going to like either 1 of them. Ebony saw trouble. 4 pains in the ass for her love, Ajay. She was only thinking of the fact that she never wanted any other man in her presence. She had no idea about their legacy. Neither of them knew the family war side of it and that was by design. Only the guys were made aware of the beef and
59

not even every guy was given all the facts or details. Only the true leaders were told every single occurrence and they were given the task of when and how to relay that info to those in their circle. Chill knows of this long time rivalry and so does Ajay. Their fathers had raised them to know about the Johnson beef. They may not have known every face or relative. But whenever something negative happened with them, you can best believe their fathers and grandfathers sought out the beef link first and often times, Big Jake *was* the culprit.

The 4 infiltrators felt anxiety when they looked up and saw Chill, Ajay, June, Rich and Tank walking toward the table they were sharing with the foursome. But when Chill appeared cool about it and suggested they let the ladies finish their talk, the 4 Jake's felt like they had gotten over. Chill suggested the guys come on with him and head to JC Penney's to shop for the apartment. But Ajay wasn't going to allow Ebony out of his sight. And definitely not with the look in their eyes, the 4 guys had. Chill had already alerted some non-crew faithful, who was in the mall. He told them not to lose sight of the 4 girls and not to allow them to leave the mall with the guys. They wanted them held up until they could get back to them, if they were to attempt to leave. He didn't mind if they walked around because that was going to make it easier for the trackers to blend in and not be noticed. Even with Ajay knowing that, he still wasn't willing to lose sight of his girl, the other girls nor the 4 infiltrators. The other crew guys tried to appear like they wasn't concerned but Ajay wasn't willing to play it off. He wanted to make sure Ebony knew he wanted her out of their company and he said as much when he told her to come with him. His gut told him that was something from the families past. It was the way the guys looked at him, like he wasn't someone important. And he knew for a fact, he was very

60

important in the lives of all 4 of those girls who sat in that pit of evil, surrounded on each end and in the middle, by these 4 enemies. Who's mission was to destroy everything those 4 girls loved and held dear. Those 4 admirers whole existence was to ultimately destroy their families.

"We're taking this spot, right over here," Tank said realizing that Ajay wasn't going to leave the food court without his sister, whom he called "twin." He also knew Ajay had a good reason for not wanting to leave and it was about more than just seeing some average dudes sitting with their future wives. He saw that look in Ajay and Chill's faces. He knew then, that it was something about their legacy. The Johnson's. The shit that he had gotten to ride on before he was even a teenager. He knew Ajay was up on what to look for, much better than he was. Just like that BJ boy, who tried to ask Ebony to prom, this past year. His life isn't going to last much longer either. Ajay is going to do away with him as soon as he has *"gone away to college"* as his alibi.

But back to the present matter. The crew sat across from the foursome and ordered food. They watched how antsy everything got with the 4 Jakes. Their girls was nervous, though Nina and T-baby tried to appear calm. The whole while, Ajay was trying to figure out how he would let Ebony know those guys were dangerous without really telling her how he knew they were. Surely she was going to want to know how he knew this and why he was so sure. He wasn't going to risk that but he was going to make his point known. She knows he has her safety on his mind, 1st and foremost. He'll make her stay away from those Jakes. And no matter how angry her girls say they are with their guys, they won't be able to pull Ebony along. Ajay knows his girl is the voice of reason, in the foursome, just as she knows he is with their boyfriends. So he's

61

going to do whatever it takes to save her and she'll be able to save them.

Meanwhile, the 4 guys big Jake had sent, went on introducing themselves to the foursome. Their names was Craig, Justin, Roger and Tim. Carl was a bit to old to try and pull himself off as a guy who wanted to date a high school girl, so they brought in Roger Pittman, who was also from Bedford Heights. Carl and Craig had championed Timothy Murphy, a new student at CSU, who had come in from Cincinnati. Justin Warner is a cousin of the now deceased Danny and Eddie Washington. Roger Pittman is on the football team with Justin, Tim and Craig.

Before long the girls got so uncomfortable with their guys watching them talk to strangers, that they got up to walk around the mall. Not to be outdone, Rich and June hopped up from their booth and went behind them. Chill, Ajay and Tank went, as well. Chill had been on the phone, the entire time. He had the streets checking into the 4 guys. Before the end of that day, he would know nearly everything there was to know about them. However, their link to big Jake was better camouflage than in the past. Big Jake had counted on that.

Ajay hadn't counted on Ebony going along with her 1st cousin and his sister's wishes to meet these guys at the movies but she had. She was the only 1 with a car. She wasn't going to be okay with them going with these new guys and she knew they wanted her to allow them to have some type of payback, for being cheated on. Still, if these girls had known what kind of danger this was, that would've thwarted the whole plot. But that's not how the crew men played it. Their motto is: *The test of being a real crew man is to have the type of control and dominance in your relationship and household, if you're in the same house, that you don't have to give your girl a reason for*
62

*why she shouldn't do something. Just her man telling her not to do it, is suppose to be enough to insure that she doesn't.*
Some of the guys took that to mean they should be able to do whatever they pleased and their girl was just going to sit tight. But today, they saw that, that wasn't the case. That was an understanding that Ajay had with Ebony, for the most part. Tank, June and Rich, not so much.

Although Rich is a Williams man, he isn't seen as 1 of the stronger men in the crew. His father wasn't viewed in that way either. They were both attracted to very strong women, by nature and T-baby was definitely strong willed. The fact that Rich and the guys had cheated on them during spring break, was the reason her and Nina was pushing what they said was their newfound freedom. Chill and Ajay was simply going to place safety nets around them and try to get Rich, Tank and June on their level. Before it was too late. As for Ebony, she was the girl Ajay loved and as long as Ebony remained truthful with Ajay, he would be able to keep her safe. Even when she didn't even know he was. Ebony was going to tell him whatever her and her girl's did or was going to do. She may beat around the bush with the particulars. But she wanted all the crew couples to stay together, so she wasn't going to make it easy for her girls to see the Jakes. It was because of that fact, Ajay and Chill would be able to keep them out of harms way.

Ajay never expected Ebony would accept a date with a bunch of strangers. But when big Greg, who is T-baby's father, called Chill's home and told them the girls had been on his home phone talking to someone with a number he didn't recognize and he redialed it, there was a male named Craig who that answered, thinking he was T-baby, calling him back. Greg had taken the number off the caller ID and passed it on to Chill, after the girls left out the house and pulled away in

63

## MORE THAN 4 ADMIRERS-RELOADED

Ebony's car. Once Ajay found out they had been on the phone with the Jakes, he knew he had to get to Ebony, right away. Big Greg had stressed it. Plus he called big Al and told him to be sure that the guys stay up with the foursome, all day. Once big Greg found out the foursome was being groomed by 4 Jakes, he wasn't okay just waiting on anyone else to handle it. But the crew rules were set in stone. Al got the word to Ajay and Chill, though they already knew about it. But allowing Chill's crew to handle this alone, was going to prove to be the hardest thing either of their fathers had ever done. Still, the rules are rules.

Nina and T-baby had made the agreement for all 4 of them to meet the 4 Jakes at Richmond Town Square cinema, for a matinee to see, *Batman Returns*. Chill had put a tail on them at the mall and that tail stayed on them, all the way to T-baby's house and back to the movie. Ajay, Chill and the guys headed back to the mall and waited outside. Ajay was pissed, just seeing her car in the parking lot. Him and Chill sent the 8 spies inside to watch them. The spies sat all around the foursome and the 4 Jakes. Neither of them even knew it.

After the movies, they went to Pizza hut. Still the spies went in while the crew waited in hiding. Inside the pizza joint, their seating arrangement was pretty much the same as the movie. Except Tim sat across from Ebony at the table. Still Ebony wouldn't make eye contact with him. Her and Rebbie was ready to leave after the pizza's arrived.

As the girls were leaving, Tim tried to step to Ebony and give her a hug. Ajay could clearly see her put her hand in his chest and shake her head. She prevented him from getting within arms reach of her. The same way it was at the movie, where she sat between T-baby and Rebbie, when she *was*

64

actually seated. The majority of the time, her and her girls was playing arcade games or was in the restroom. While they was playing arcade games, their guys could see them. Because the arcade was out in the very front lobby of theatre. Still Ajay was antsy because she went. As he watched her, she looked as if she was trying to convince Nina and T-baby to just leave the guys inside the theatre and leave the movie. But they was bucking against her. She reluctantly followed them back inside the movie, looking over her shoulder the whole way.

"I feel like twin know we're out here," Tank had said.

"No," Chill said, "She doesn't wanna be there."

"I'm gonna make sure she don't do this again," Ajay said, "I know that shit. Tank y'all gonna have to get y'all shit right. Because these girls are targets. We can't let them go off like this, knowing the shit we know."

Ajay was angry at everything and everybody, at that point. If Ebony was to be harmed, that would make him a failure in his heart and mind.

"Get y'all situations *right*, man," he repeated, "I'm gonna handle mine, once and for all. This shit will not happen again."

After another 20 minutes and the foursome was back in the lobby. Ebony was again trying to convince Nina and T-baby of something and they were still defiant. At that point, it became hard for Ajay not to make her aware that he was there.

"Chill, I just wish I could tell her what the real reasons are for me not wanting her to go somewhere like this," he said, "Because I know she's not gonna cheat. But if she knew, then she would understand why she can't just go off with just *anybody*. She could communicate that to her girls."

"I hear you," Chill said, "But she would also live her life in fear and she wouldn't ever be okay with you going anywhere either. I feel that's why the fathers never went into

65

detail with the females. Because they would worry themselves to death and we wouldn't ever be able to leave the house, even to handle business. Not without them worrying that we're gonna be killed or that we're out killing."

"I know I'm gonna kill *these* motherfuckahz," Ajay said, "I'm looking forward to it too. I mean that old ass man is on my last nerve. He wanna come at my future *wife*?! That old bitch really wants to ruin me. I swear I'm gonna have to cut off his damn arm and let him lay there and bleed out."
Chill and the other guys laughed but Ajay didn't. He had plans of doing exactly what he'd just said. He's totally offended that someone would send another guy to harm his girl. Especially after the shit she'd already gone through in Houston.
"I'm knocking him off," Ajay said, "Believe that shit."

After they returned from the matinee and eating pizza, the girls went back to T-baby's house, only to hear that Pearl had been trying to find Ebony. They all thought the guys had told what they saw at the mall. After telling Greg and Sandy where they were going, they headed to Pearl's house.

Ajay and Ebony talked briefly in his families side of the shed. He wanted Ebony to come with him to his apartment. He had plans of telling her enough to make her understand the type of danger those guys were. After all, he was leaving for college in a month. He couldn't go off with this thing lingering. Once Pearl was done talking, Ebony and Ajay headed to his apartment. He had gotten a spot out there near Arthur Owens. The same apartments where they had killed Lil Jake. At the time he moved there, the 4 Jakes wasn't tenants. But it wouldn't be long before they would get an apartment there too. When they did move in, they got a unit perpendicular to his, so they could see his front door. He knew that was done

66

intentionally and he welcomed it. He looked forward to their day of reckoning.

Ajay and Ebony arrived at his spot. He steps inside first, then holds the door for her to come in. He could see Arthur, Kilo and Wayne watching them as they went in. He knew they would be on the lookout until they left heading back to Shaker Heights. Ebony hadn't seen the inside of the apartment which was suppose to be half hers. Not until that night. That made Ajay sad. He had lived there for a week and she hadn't even been over. Primarily because she found out that he had an orgy at the motel during spring break. Him, Tank, June and Rich tricked with 4 of the stigmatic ho's, known to set the foursome's temperatures at blazing. That's the reason Nina and T-baby had been pretending to want another, when that's the farthest thing from the truth. She knew they didn't want to be single, no more than she did. She had never considered her and Ajay's relationship to be over. She first claimed they was on a hiatus until he lived up to her demands. But she still hooked up with him at Chill's, Arthur's or Rob's, because she was in love with the way it felt when his hands touched her. His lips too. She was addicted to him, just as he was to her. The only problem was, she wasn't willing to share the thorough loving making she received from him, with anyone else. She figured he would understand that since he couldn't even stand to know that a guy lusted after her. Only Ajay knew the Jakes wasn't about lust. It was much worse.

She was at his apartment and she knew the evening wouldn't end without sex. She planned on it being great sex, which she knew she'd get because that was what he prided himself on. She had refused to come to his spot, out of defiance because he had given her loving away. She expected him to be anxious to make love since tonight would be their 1st time in

67

his new place. In her mind, she was there, 1st and foremost to get some answers. 2$^{nd}$, to get several orgasms. Even though she was still to shy to say the word in front of him. Her main concern was why had he been sharing hers with others, when he was so dead set on making sure that she understood that his wasn't even to be approached. It angered him to know another guy had lust for her. She had told him they needed to talk and he'd agreed too. He looked ready to give her the answers she sought. Based on his mannerisms and questions, she had started to feel like maybe he had witnessed her and her girls earlier outing. She just couldn't be sure. Still she was determined to try and dictate the topics. He wanted to get cozy. She challenged him. That shifted the power his way, where it had really never left. She was prepared to have him to answer as to why he had fucked Angel, Alana, Tameka, Nicole and Angie, in an orgy session at the motel. But she hadn't realized yet, that she would be the one on the hot seat before it was all said and done.

"Come sit on the couch with me," he said calmly after giving her a cool drink.

She moved over next to him. He had already taken off his shirt and shoes. He lit 1 of his blunts from a stash he'd rolled earlier. She complimented the look of the apartment but he was only thinking of her and how unsafe she was earlier. Still he had to stay within the rules. The *male* rules.

"I had all this set up for us, for a week," he said, showing her the wine, Hennessy, foods and the movies he'd bought.

"I wanted us to spend all summer together but you're telling me to let my boys hang out over here. What does that sound like to you?"

"I don't know," she said.

He hit the blunt, then gave her a shotgun from it. Afterwards, 68 he laid it in the ashtray and sat his drink down. He pulled her close to him and started kissing her, while rubbing his hands through her hair. He wanted some of her loving, so he could clear his mind. The only way he could do that was to hold her close to him and feel her heartbeat. He knew he could make her understand that she just wasn't going to be allowed to be around those guys, if he could just hold her. If he could make love to her while whispering into her ear, how much he loves and needs for her not to divide his time, he could get her to commit to not supporting her girls, on any future missions of hanging out with the Jakes. But she wanted to wear the pants. She wanted to control the conversation, instead of being who she was, his submissive princess. She decided she wanted to be, that Nina or T-baby kind of stubborn. She was bucking against him even though she knew she had been out with another man. One who had plans of killing her man and possibly her too. She was refusing to allow things to happen naturally. She kept asking him to talk. He wanted to make love. She wanted to be the man. He lost it. It wasn't until then that she realized he knew she had been out with the guys, he saw sitting with her at the mall. After she learned her game was up, she finally got quiet. That was a little too late. He started asking all of the important questions and his tone dared her to lie so she told the complete truth.

Afterwards he laid down the law and told her it wasn't going to happen again. Or he would make her father aware that she'd gone out with a boy she didn't even know.

"Okay," she said, "I won't. Please don't tell my daddy."

"I don't wanna discuss that shit, no more," he told her, "I'm taking your shit off and you're gonna fuck me. Since you got time to go out with some nigga you don't even know. You ought to be good and hot for me, by now, Miss Ebony Brown.

69

I know I'm hot for you and I have been. But you had plans, ha? Show me what you got for me. Since it was none of that kind of talk going on wit them bitch ass niggaz, tonight."

"It wasn't Anthony, I promise," she said because she knew there was some punishment coming as she stood up.

"Let's get you naked," he said as he started to undress her, "You can promise me that way. I'm ready to fuck my girl and you already know you're gonna pay me for lying to me in the shed. Do you understand me?"

"Yes," is all she said as she stood still and exhaled.

She had gone on a date with an enemy, though she didn't know that part. The whole point was, she was raised to know better then to go anywhere with a stranger. Furthermore, she has a man. A *Jackson* man. Whom she knows would never stand for his woman to be in the company of another man who has desires for her. That's what she thought the 4 Jakes was about. Yet she still went.

"I'm gonna punish this pussy tonight, Ebony," he said, "That's the only way I can whoop your ass and feel good about it. You don't take my pussy around no nigga, baby girl. You're gonna learn that tonight. And I'm trying to fuck all night too."

His mind was made up and his dick was extra hard. She was the only person who could make him do something different, after he'd made up his mind. But even she couldn't change his mind about going hard on her, that night. He removed all of her clothes as he looked from her body to her eyes and back to her body. While he felt her up, at the same time.

"I just wanna make sure everything is like it was when I last held it. Come on down here," he said as he pulled her down to the couch with him and immediately flipped her onto her back. He had his knees on the couch, spread apart, while his toes pointed toward the floor. He lifted her ass up to him and

70

entered her swiftly. The only part of her body that was still touching the couch was her head and shoulders. He stood and put his feet on the floor where he could look directly down at her face. She could see his too but she was afraid to look at him. She knew she was in trouble.

"I'm sorry, Anthony," she tried.

It hurt him to know she would go against him, for her girls. That's some shit that cannot be allowed to happen again, if he was going to be the man of his house. She would have to learn that night and she would have to know when he told her to do something, there was no other option.

"My pussy must be extra hot, ha?" he asked but didn't really care if she answered.

He said, "It must be for you to be going out with a nigga, knowing I'm looking for you to come see me. Hell yea, this motherfuckah hot and you know Ajay ain't never gonna share his pussy wit nobody. You know that shit already. Don't you baby girl? Ha?"

He pounded her with force, right there on his couch. He didn't bother to start slow. He went for the kill, immediately. He was slamming his 13 inches into her, like she asked for it that way.

"Oh Anthony!" she screamed.

"And that's the only motherfuckin name you need to remember, baby girl," he said as he pounded her some more.

He was very angry. But he was also afraid that she wasn't getting the message of how important it was that she obeyed him. He was going to keep her from harm, if she would only listen to him.

"I ain't about to share you, Ebony!" he yelled as he fucked her even harder.

"Okay!" she screamed, "Oh God!"

He pulled her around and laid her on the couch. He laid down

71

on top of her and continue the slamming his dick into her tight pussy. She could see the anger in his eyes but there was more than just anger. She knew he was trying to make a point.

"I understand you, baby!" she screamed her plea, "I'm sorry! I want do that no more! Okay?! Okay?! Oh please!"

He wants to quiet her because he isn't done punishing her. He wasn't even close to being done with shelling out her lesson. She started to cry but he wasn't in the mood to sympathize with her. He wanted to fuck her, well enough. So that the next time she was faced with an issue like that and thought of defying him. She would get a pain *so sharp* in and around her pelvic area, that it would shoot straight down through her pussy, causing her to have to pin her knees together and take a seat. She grimaced in pain. He grimaced to get more leverage, so he could push it to the limit. Suddenly he reached for the back of her head and brought her face to his. He jammed his tongue into her mouth like a starved maniac. It was like he couldn't kiss her hard enough to make her see that he wanted her. She had tried to keep him close to her and kissing her because he wasn't pounding her as hard then. But he released her lips, as if he knew what her thoughts was. He seemed angry that he liked the kissing part. He wasn't ready to please her yet. He rolled his eyes at her, as he went for her breast and started sucking her nipples. He was sucking on each one, as if he was getting a sweet taste that got sweeter with a harder pull. Her pussy was already hurting and now even her nipples were sore. Only because he wanted them to be.

"Oh baby!" she screamed, "Pleasssssssee!"

"I do, God dammit!" he yelled back to her, "And that's what you're gonna do too. You're gonna please your man. Fuck what anybody else wanna do or want you to do! Do you hear me, baby!?! Do you understand me?! Ha?!"

72

## MORE THAN 4 ADMIRERS-RELOADED

"Yes, Anthony! I'm sorry!"

"Not yet, you're not," he whispered suddenly, "I'm swelling my motherfuckin pussy shut, tonight. Maybe then you can chill the fuck out. This is *my* shit. I've told you that enough times for you to know it by now. You're gonna act like you know this is mine, by the time I let you up out o' here."

"I know it's yours Anthony!" she tried as she cried, "I would never give it away!"

"And you're not gonna take it around no nigga either, baby," he oozed, "Do you hear me? Ha?"

"Okay! Okay!"

But he's just getting started. There's no stopping in him, for at least another 3 hours. He even took catnaps in between fucking and came back to it, a few more times. He did it twice on the couch. Then on the floor in front of the couch. She thought moving away from him would curtail his desire but that didn't work. She slipped into the bathroom and was going to wash up before going home. He fucked her in there, even harder and with more conversation. He told her she wasn't leaving yet.

"Not tonight," he said, "You're staying with me until we wake up. Big John knows where you're at. He'll tell mama Pearl. So far, he don't know what y'all did. None of y'all father's do. But they can find out, if that's what you want, baby girl."

It was only after he'd fucked her in 4 different spots in the apartment, the final time being in his bed, that he let her get some sleep. It was nearly 4am when he rested his case. She was beat and so was her pussy. Literally. She laid curled up in the fetal position. Her body quivered like she was lying on a glacier. He laid down behind her and watched as she cowered to him. Afraid to even move because that might set him off again. She knew for sure, she wasn't ever going around those

73

guys anymore. Nor any other guys, for that matter. Ever again in her life. She couldn't stand for her man to be angry with her. When he was, he took it out on her vagina and it just wasn't as grown as his dick was. He was going to turn 18 in a few weeks but his dick had been grown for years. Her 17$^{th}$ birthday is still 6 months away. But she feels like she'll never handle her man's penis size. He's laid up behind her, planting sweet kisses on her shoulders and the back of her neck. While he's talking about registering to vote on his birthday. All the while she was just praying to God that nothing about voting made him horny because her pussy felt like it was hanging off of her body, at that point.

Later when he did tell her he was ready to take her to Shaker Heights and she started to get up, he told her to lay back down. He was going to run her bath and he was going to bath her too.

"It's okay, baby," she said, her voice hoarse from screaming for mercy, all night, "I can do it."

"I'm quite sure you can," he said, "but I want too. Just the bath, for now."

He said he had plans for them tonight and he was looking forward to it.

"Are you gonna come up with some excuse as to why you can't come see me tonight?" he asked, just to get a measure of how well the lesson went.

"All I need to know is what time you wanna hook up," she said, keeping her voice soft and non-confrontational.

"Tank's gonna use your car," he said, "I'm picking you up when we go to the courts, so we'll just go from there."

"Okay, baby," she whispered.

He felt sorry for her, at this point, But he wasn't going to let up. She was sorry she defied him. He could tell that much. But

74

## MORE THAN 4 ADMIRERS-RELOADED

She knew after last night and from this day forward, going out somewhere with non-crew guys was definitely not going to be apart of her life. Ajay's case was closed and his point made was made.

****Update up to and after> Time To Love-part 3****

Big Jake's beef hasn't ended. Each of his seek-and-destroy-the-crew missions have failed, 99% of the time. He didn't learn nearly as well as Ebony did, when the lesson was there for him. He had tried to divide and conquer the crew, way back when Allen Saul and Allen Sr was the leaders. It failed him miserably. He still hasn't given up and he won't. Not until he's dead. But going after Ebony had proven to be a waste of time. Tim got his ass whooped and Ajay got shot in the process. Afterwards, Tim and the few Jakes who were still lucky enough to have their lives, moved out of University Heights and transferred to another Cleveland State Campus at Lakeland Community College, in Kirkland. That's only 22 miles east of Cleveland. That ain't nearly far enough to keep Chill, Ajay and the crew off of their asses. For now, they've got their payroll law enforcement officers tailing and tagging them. One of those officers who was also Ajay's parole officer, at one point, had been on the hook since the days of big Paul. That officer had helped Chester Lee tamper with evidence to make it look as if he had killed Jake Jr in 1985, as well. Chester is doing his time but he will walk free again. This officer had helped Al and John kill Jake Jr and he was the prosecutor's primary witness during Chester Lee's trial. Wheeler and Parkwood set it up, that way. Chester Lee will be free from Federal prison before his granddaughter Chastity Jaquel or CJ, gets done with high school.

75

# MORE THAN 4 ADMIRERS-RELOADED

Chill, Ajay and their crew have the beads on big Jake's accomplices. They've killed Carl and Craig. Justin, Tim and Roger are living on borrowed time. BJ the football player isn't going to grow any older either. The crew are just bidding their time before all of the Jakes meet their maker.

These days, Chill's crew have wives and/or families and a lot more to lose. Ajay, June and Rich are professional athletes who have invested their salaries well. But none as well as Ajay. They live in a secluded and upscale community which they named: *Jackson Heights*. A gated and secured community with 24 hour guard service and surveillance. They have also turned that 8 suite strip mall into a U-shaped money making machine of 24 suites. Plus a detail shop with jobs and businesses for all 3 generations. They named it *CrewLand mall*. They are living the dream their forefathers and mothers attempted. There's no stopping the drive of this Cleveland crew, in any generation. I wouldn't suggest you try.

### *Points to take from this story*

For the big Jake's of the world, there is a lesson to be learned here. First and foremost, stay to your own and get your own. Make a way in your community that allows you all to feed yourselves and put money back into it. In other words, make it possible to spend and make your money in the same place. But if you spend your life trying to hinder a thinking man or woman, you will forever lose.

*Why would you even want to tear another human being down, who has only tried to better you?*

There is something absolutely race killing about the crab-in-the-barrel mentality. If your sister, brother or an entire clan of

76

people are doing well for themselves. And they're not taking anything from you to accomplish this. Then why is it that we, as Black folks, can't be supportive and thrilled for them?

Big Jake had the problem of thinking that someone owed him something, when that was not a reality. He could've worked hard and flourished, right along with the crew. Because like Allen Sr told him, he was only going to take care of his wife and children, just like every other man in his crew. He told big Jake to be his own man.

So I guess, just like many males today, big Jake either never learned how to be his own man, never wanted to be his own man or he got caught up in this idiotic position of thinking that somehow the government and/or the world, owed him something because of slavery. That's absolutely ridiculous and it's the farthest thing from what a real black man is.

Get yours, like the crew does it. And keep it amongst your hard working brothers and sisters. Take care of each other and raise each others children to be strong and self sufficient and not race killers. That's the only way our communities, cities, states, Country and our children's future, will survive.

One Love,
Author Black Coffee
www.truesrelatepublishing.com

---

Get other short stories in this
Time Will Reveal series by Black Coffee

# The Time Will Reveal short stories

---

**#1 MORE THAN 4 ADMIRERS-RELOADED**
**#2 MR. WRONG AND THE RATS-RELOADED**
**#3 THE CREW'S PRIORITY [TBD]**

# The Time Will Reveal, the novel series

Time To Learn-RELOADED-part 1
Time To Grow-RELOADED-part 2
Time To Love-RELOADED-part 3
Time To Know-RELOADED-part 4
Time To Feel-RELOADED-part 5
The Making of AJAY-Every Man (Print only)
Time To Show-part 6 [TBD]
Ajay and Ebony 1-Time Will Reveal 7-Time To Give [TBD]
Ajay and Ebony 2-Time Will Reveal 8-Time To Live [TBD]

And see more novels by Black Coffee at:
www.truesrelatepublishing.com
www.blackdollone.com

Join us on Facebook at:
Group: Black Coffee's Crew Nation
Fan Page: Black Coffee's Books

78

www.ingramcontent.com/pod-product-compliance
Lightning Source LLC
Chambersburg PA
CBHW070539130626
46555CB00003B/1497